Mama B: A Time to Love
Novella #3 in the Mama B Series
by Michelle Stimpson

*IF.*
*Stimpson*

Published by MLStimpson Enterprises
MichelleStimpson.com
Michelle@MichelleStimpson.com

Cover and design by Delia Latham
Deliadesigns.webs.com

With love and appreciate to the readers
who encourage me daily.
Thank you, thank you, thank you!

# Acknowledgments

Thanks be to God for His special work in me as I wrote this book. He has brought me into a greater revelation of His love for us, and I am forever grateful. A thousand years from now, we will still sing of His great love.

Thanks to fellow authors April Dishon Barker and L.A. Logan for being a sounding board for this book. I had my thoughts, too, but the final product came out very different from what even I knew! God is good.

Thanks again to my writing group for their thoughts and encouragement with Mama B. We didn't get to do much together this go-round, but I certainly felt your prayers!

My family always makes a bit of a sacrifice when I'm writing a book. The love and support of those closest to me is invaluable. Love you!

Finally, to those who help with the finishing touches – Delia (cover art) and Karen Rodgers (editing) – your eyes and skills are a blessing to me!

# Chapter 1

One good thing about volunteering at the food pantry is you never forget to be thankful for every scrap of food that finds its way to your own plate. I done seen folk come in wearing all kind of hundred-dollar shirts, totin' thousand-dollar purses. Pink slips and middle-age-crisis-havin' husbands don't care what all kind of help you were last year or last week. With one bad report on a computer screen or one good swish of the new secretary's hips, honey, many-a-woman has found herself in need of a hot meal.

I suppose I shouldn't make it seem like it was only women coming to the pantry. Say 95% was women. The rest was men, mostly on drugs, and there was a few people I couldn't tell if they was standin' or squattin'.

Don't matter, though, since we all God's creation. That was my attitude about serving folk at the center. I didn't care what they look like or whatever brought them there—everybody needs to eat, especially the babies. Even though the government help we got there had a bunch of rules, I couldn't bring myself to turn away nobody who was hungry.

But they had done sent out a note to every center, which the new location director, Rhonda Hall, read to everyone the previous week. "Due to budget cuts and redistricting, we must follow the guidelines as outlined in the center handbook, including the jurisdictional stipulations."

Me and Libby just looked at each other and rolled our eyes. I support the President and the country and all, but some of them rules don't make no sense and everybody knows it. Plus, they keep changing 'em every time you look up.

Anyhow, we made it through almost a whole week before the new rules got tested. It was Friday, around a quarter 'til four. We was all straightening things up, emptying the kitchen trash cans and sweeping the floors so we could close up for the weekend. Me and Libby always did an extra-strong cleaning, since sometimes we didn't make it back for a couple of weeks, with the center hours being reduced and all.

In comes a woman we hadn't seen in a while. She real big, always wearing shorts and flip flops no matter what the weather, that's how I know she got varicose veins real bad in one leg. I suppose them veins had something to do with the cane she carried. She had wild, curly brown hair and a nose to where you could tell that even though she looked white, she got some black or Indian in her somewhere down the line. Like I said, don't make me no difference what folk look like, I'm just sayin' this is how I recognized her. I couldn't remember her name, but her voice was etched in my mind forever, too—real proper, loud and raspy all at the same time.

"Helloooooo there!" the woman called in her distinct tone.

Libby looked up and smiled at me. We both stepped back further into the kitchen area because we knew Miss Hall and the new rules was about to meet their match.

I heard Rhonda's heels cross the few feet from her desk to the greeting counter. "How can I help you?"

"I need an emergency food pack, please."

Me and Libby peeked out the kitchen to watch.

"Well, our emergency food packs are for extenuating circumstances only. Do you have an urgent situation?"

The patron squinted up at Rhonda. "Yes. I'm hungry."

Rhonda grabbed a few forms and a pen from under the counter and presented them to the woman. "You can fill these out and—"she looked at her watch—"bring them back Monday morning." She held out the forms for the woman to take with her.

The woman propped one hand on her hip and used the other to tap her cane on the floor. "Are you pulling my leg?"

Libby elbowed me in the side. I tried to poke her back, but she squirmed out of reach, giggling softly as we continued to watch the mess unfold.

"No," Rhonda held her ground. "We have new rules. They've been posted on the outside window for a week now."

"Well, I haven't been here in more than a week. I usually go to the one over in Mesquite. It's closer to me. But since I was out this way at the thrift shop—"

Rhonda shook her head and retracted the papers. "Oh, if you live closer to that location, you're out of our jurisdiction. We can't serve you here. You need to go *there*."

"But they'll be closed by the time I get back!"

"I'm sorry. There's nothing we can do for you here."

"Sweetheart, how old are you?" the woman asked Rhonda.

"Twenty-three," Miss Rhonda smacked.

"Honey, I've got *underwear* older than you and I've paid enough taxes to cover your salary for the next ten years. Now, I'm hungry and I'm not going anywhere else to get my food."

That's when Libby rushed to the refrigerator and snatched one of those emergency packs off the top tray. She pulled me in for the intervention. This drama had gone on long enough.

"Hello, Eunice."

I was glad Libby remembered her name.

"Finally. Here's somebody with half a brain," Eunice sighed at the sight of us. "Hi, Libby."

"Hey. You remember my friend, Beatrice? We call her B."

"Yes. Good to see you again, B." Eunice gave me a hearty smile.

Libby set the recyclable grocery bag on the counter, but Rhonda grabbed the handles and set it on our side of the divider. She looked Libby dead in her eyes. "No, Miss Libby. We cannot give her this food."

"Miss Eunice now understands that she has to go to the other center," I jumped in. "I'm sure she won't come here again. But today, this one time, won't hurt." I grabbed the sack handles and attempted to transfer the sack again, but I tell you Miss Rhonda jerked that thing away from me so hard my elbow like ta popped out the socket!

"Rhonda!" Libby shrieked.

"Is you crazy, pulling my arm like that?" I fussed. *This girl need some anger management classes.*

"No!" Rhonda exploded. "She is *not* getting this sack!"

Next thing I know, Eunice's cane come swinging from across that counter. Rhonda saw it and ducked in time. Libby wasn't so quick. The rubber tip caught her right on the cheek. Instantly, a red streak appeared on Libby's face.

Libby's hand covered the spot as she hollered, "Stop it!"

"I'm so sorry!" Eunice squealed, trying to hop over the barrier, which could not have happened seeing as she was probably close to two hundred fifty pounds and only had one good leg. In her panic, she musta thought she was gonna get some extra strength, like the mommas who pick up cars off their babies. Clearly she wasn't gettin' no such extra help from on high at the moment.

Chile, this was sho' 'nuff a sad scene. Got Libby on one side holding on to her cheek, Eunice lookin' like a broke-down Spiderman, and Rhonda shakin' like a leaf talkin' on her cell phone.

"Eunice, get down before you hurt yourself," I ordered. "You all right, Libby?"

Libby twitched her chin from left to right. "I think so."

"Here, let me look at you." I slanted her face a little to the right. Didn't look too bad, as far as the scratch went, but she was sure gon' have a bad bruise in the morning. "Put some ice on it when you get home."

With Libby checked out and both of Eunice's feet back on the ground, look like my mind could finally process what Rhonda was doing. By that point, she'd already ended her unnecessary phone call.

"The police are on the way."

# Chapter 2

"What you call the police for?" I asked.

"She assaulted me!" Rhonda yelled.

"That woman did not hit you."

"She *tried* to hit me."

"But she missed," I corrected Rhonda.

Eunice finally got that extra power as she swiveled and made double-time toward the door. Rhonda shot out from the safety of the counter and twisted that door lock before Eunice could reach the exit. Then she took the long route back to the safety of her desk. "You're not leaving until the cops get here."

A part of me wished Eunice had of escaped, but I knew it was best for her to stay there and wait until the police cleared her to leave because Rhonda probably wasn't gonna let it go. She'd have Eunice on *America's Most Wanted*, left up to her.

"Eunice, you might best just wait here." I pointed to the wooden bench underneath the community bulletin board.

Libby shuffled out the kitchen area with an ice pack pressed to her face. She strong. *Thank you, Lord.*

Eunice hoisted herself up from the bench and took the last few steps to meet Libby. "I am so sorry. You know I wasn't trying to hit you, right?"

"Yes, Eunice. I know. It was an accident. Kinda."

Eunice poked her cane in Rhonda's direction. "I meant to hit *her*."

"Well, you didn't really need to hit anyone," Libby scolded.

Eunice yelled toward Rhonda, "It's not your food, anyway! It's the government's! It belongs to everyone!"

"Tell that to the police," Rhonda smarted off. But she didn't take one step toward Eunice again, that's for sure.

We all waited until the officers arrived. I was hoping they would just tell everybody to cool down and go home. I already knew Libby wasn't going to press no charges. She not the type of person to go by the letter of the law, which is exactly what got us in that position to begin with, I reckon.

But when the officer asked Eunice for her ID, we ran into a bit of a problem. She got some kind of little fine she hadn't paid. "Ma'am, you're going to have to come with us."

"I got the money to pay it right here," Eunice said, patting her fanny pack.

"I'm sorry, but you'll have to handle this downtown."

And with that, they put those little plastic strings on Miss Eunice's wrists and led her toward the front door. That Eunice let out a holler that would have raised a thousand dollars for charity. "I'm sorry. I was just hungry. I didn't do anything wrong," she wailed.

I looked back at Rhonda, who had somehow managed to stay glued to her seat nearly the whole time Libby and I had been trying to explain this whole mishap to the police, begging for mercy on Eunice's behalf.

"Libby, call my son, Judge Paul Lemon. Dallas County."

Ooh, Rhonda's eyes got real big then. "Your son's a *judge*?"

"Yes," Eunice sniffed. "He works downtown, presides over criminal cases. He locks up tons of bad guys and throws away the key."

The officer who'd been prodding Eunice forward stopped. "Ummm...ma'am...we...do appreciate it when the courts validate all our hard work. Do you want to call your son *first*?"

Hmph. Aint' that something? Every once in a while them politics works in your favor.

"Okay," Eunice huffed again, straining her neck so she could wipe her nose on her shirt. She'd cleared up that crying awful quick-like. Made me wonder if she was putting on a show, if her son really was in the position she claimed he was in. If not, she had done worked up an extra helping of trouble with those fine officers.

Eunice rattled off a telephone number to Libby, who dialed on Eunice's behalf, seeing as Eunice's hands were still behind her back. "Yes, this is Mrs. Libby Maxwell. I need to speak to Judge Lemon, please...No, I can't leave a message. Tell him it's regarding his mother...Yes, I'll hold."

Libby played that Momma card real nice, and within a few moments, she and the oldest officer had negotiated so Eunice's twist ties came off. There was some winking and some unspoken understandings I knew Libby would catch me up on later. But for the moment, Eunice was released into the custody of Libby, with the agreement Eunice would handle the fine first thing Monday morning and only seek help from the correct food pantry. Whew! What a mess, all over a sack of free food!

The officers apologized for restraining Eunice. Eunice apologized again for hitting Libby. Me and Libby apologized for involving them in such a petty matter when they could have been out stopping a real criminal.

The only person who didn't offer no kind of remorse was Rhonda. She kept fiddling with her keys, twirling them kinky strings on her head like she do every time she get nervous about one of the homeless people with a mental problem.

Only, she didn't look scared. She was mad 'cause all ended well. That's just like the enemy, though. He don't like to see nobody get mercy 'cause God ain't gon' give him none when it's all said and done.

Soon as the officers left, Rhonda grabbed her fake Coach bag and stomped toward the doors to lead the way out.

"Goodnight," Libby spoke for me and Eunice, too.

Rhonda didn't say nothing else. When we got outside, she pulled the doors to, twisted that key to lock them, and hopped into her Kia with the BMW emblem on the front. *She* the one need to be investigated with all that bootleg merchandise, if you ask me.

# Chapter 3

"Oh shoot," Eunice gushed angrily, "I've missed my ride back home."

"You want me to call 'em for you?" Libby asked.

Eunice shook her head. "I don't know her name or her number. I just hitched a ride to Peasner with her. Told her I'd meet her back at the gas station on Main by four so we could ride back into the city. Didn't know I was going to get held up here. I'm sure she's gone by now."

I could hardly believe my ears. "You rode here with a total stranger?"

"She was nice. Had two little kids in the car. She said I reminded her of her own mother." Eunice smiled. "Plus I gave her gas money. Fifty dollars, which was more than enough to get us here and back."

Libby lectured, "Eunice, women our age can't go around hitch-hikin' and pullin' cash money out of our pocketbooks in front of people we don't know!"

Eunice shrugged. "Well, I've had a few incidents, but I've been okay so far."

"By the grace of God," I let her know.

Eunice nodded. "Probably so." She led the way outside. Without looking down, she reached into her fanny pack, pulled out a cigarette and a lighter. Seem like in one motion, she lit it, stuck it in her mouth, and took a long puff to get it going. She turned her head to the side and blew the smoke away from Libby and me. "Looks like I won't be coming to this center anymore. So, thank you both for sticking your necks out for me with the youngster and with the police. We old ladies have to look out for each other sometimes."

Eunice swung that cane forward and started down the building steps and across the parking lot. Me and Libby stood there shocked for a second until the Holy Spirit finally gave us the sense to speak.

"Eunice," we called in unison.

She planted her cane and turned her neck toward us. "Huh?"

"We can't leave you out here," I protested, walking toward her with Libby trailing behind. "You want us to get hold of your son again?"

She waved her hand. "No. He won't come. He only puts on a show for his name's sake."

"You got any other kids? Grandkids?"

"Not in Texas. Not any that give a rat's behind about me. But that's neither here nor there. I've made it this far, I'll keep on going. Don't worry yourselves about me. You've been very helpful already. Thank you." She turned again and began her awkward stride toward the sidewalk.

Now, I know when people are puttin' on a show so you can feel sorry for 'em and offer to help. You know how they do—they mouth say one thing, but their body language and their eyes say another. They got to hold they face to the ground so them crocodile tears can slide down. Still, they got to sneak a look up at you every couple of seconds to see if you buyin' their sob story.

But that wasn't the case with Eunice. I got a good feelin' if me and Libby had let her walk away, she wouldn't have turned back, not once. As I watched her hobble onto the sidewalk, the Holy Spirit started pinching my heart.

To be honest, I was waiting on Him to pinch Libby's heart harder than mine so she could be the one to do all the reachin' out. I mean, she the one married to a preacher. She the one actually remembered Eunice's name. Plus, I didn't have no intentions on driving Eunice home to Mesquite that night. I had other plans.

Eunice kept on hobbling down that road.

"B, we have to do something," Libby whispered to me.

*We?* Didn't *we* just tell Eunice not to mess with strangers? That same rule should have applied to me and Libby, too.

Eunice's body was getting smaller and smaller in my vision. "I can't take her back home. I got things to do."

"I sure can't. My cheek's puffing up. I got to get home and get some ice before the swelling makes it up to my eye and I can't even see," she informed me.

One look at her confirmed the medical situation.

"Libby, you know me and Frank go dancing on Friday nights. I got less than an hour to get ready as it is," I nearly pleaded with her.

She blinked her normal eye. "Well, now, you and Frank been dancing every Friday for several weeks now. Seem like the world wouldn't stop turning if you missed one evening."

I wagged my finger in her face. "Watch out. You the one got me started goin' out with this man. No sense in changing your mind now." I could have added that I sensed she'd been a teenchy bit jealous about how I'd been going out more with Frank, seeing as our dating and dancing had cut back on the amount of time I spent walking and volunteering with Libby. But I kept that information to myself.

"I know, I know, B. Don't have a cow. I'm just teasin' with you. But we gotta do somethin' before she gets to the end of the block."

I took a deep breath. Libby was right. If I'd turned on the news the next morning and seen a report about Eunice found somewhere in a back alley, I'd have to fight that guilt off until the day I died. *Okay, Lord, I hear You.* "Eunice! Wait!"

# Chapter 4

Even after we finally convinced Eunice to get in our car, we still didn't have a plan. Frank and I had a standing Friday night date. Truth be told, I would have been more upset about missing it than him. The only option I could think of was Eunice going home with Libby, spending the night with her and Peter until Saturday morning. Then I'd come over and me and Libby could take Eunice home together, since Peter didn't drive no more.

But Eunice shot that idea down from the back seat of Libby's car. "Oh no, ma'am. I will not spend the night under a roof with another woman's husband. That kind of arrangement always turns out bad for me."

Me and Libby could hardly keep from laughing. If Eunice thought Peter had a mind to take a peek at her, she must have been living in 1965. Plus, Peter was slower on his cane than Eunice. But if this woman say she got a problem with other women's husbands, who was I to tell her she didn't?

"How about this," Libby suggested. "Eunice, you'll stay at my house until B gets back from her night out with Frank. Then she and Frank will pick you up from my house and take you back to B's house until tomorrow."

"Frank won't be spending the night?" Eunice quizzed.

"Oh, no. Me and Frank ain't married."

She smacked. "That don't mean nothin'."

"It means something to me," I quipped.

*Lord, what kind of person you done brought to me now?*

Frank wore his favorite dancing shoes—the black, shiny ones with brown on the tips and sides. To me, they looked like bowling shoes, but he insisted they were comfortable and made him feel like Frank Sinatra.

I suppose if he could sing, he might have something going there, but Lord knows Frank's singing voice was not meant for the public. Oh, he'd tried a few times to hum a few bars in my ear while we danced. Them off-key tunes shoulda been kept between him and Jesus.

My Albert couldn't sing, either, but that man could sho' 'nuff whistle. I ain't never heard nobody whistle *Precious Lord* and *My Soul Loves Jesus* the way Albert did. Seem like he was anointed to whistle on Sunday mornings while we was getting dressed for church.

You know, mostly it be the little piddly stuff you miss about somebody when they're gone.

When I went out with Frank, I always had my moment of remembering Albert before I kissed the past goodbye and moved on with the present. When Frank and I first started going out, I was upset about this hurdle I had to jump over every time I strapped myself into his car and smelled his unforgettable aftershave. No, he wasn't Albert. He wasn't the man I'd known, loved and trusted for over forty years.

He was Frank. And this wasn't then, this was now. The hurdle was still there, but I expected it, and I expected to jump over it. I noticed it got smaller and smaller every time we went out.

"Hello there, lovely," Frank greeted me as he opened the passenger's side door.

"Hello there, my handsome escort," I replied, stepping up into his Range Rover.

He shut my door and walked around the back of the car. In that moment, I got a short taste of the music he'd been listening to. Sounded like that Beyonce girl everybody's always rantin' and ravin' about. Every time I seen her on TV, she looked half-naked, bless her heart. Now, the girl *could* sing, but I wondered would folks like her as much if she put on some clothes.

Anyhow, I reminded myself that Frank was a grown man and he could listen to whatever he wanted to in his own car.

When he'd gotten settled back into his seat, he took it upon himself to switch the CD changer to another selection. The music of gospel artist Myron Williams came coursing out from the speakers. Inside, I smiled at Frank's respect for my preference and thanked God for teaching both of us to get over each other's differences. We both loved the Lord. Just, I was more Pentecostal-like saved and Frank was more Baptist-like. In the Bible, Paul said there was no such thing as *this* kind of Christian and *that* kind, though, so I probably needed to set it out my mind.

"You ready to cut this rug with me, B?"

"Whew! After the day I had at the food pantry, I need to dance the night away."

On the way to the studio, I told Frank all about what happened with Eunice and why we needed to pick her up from Libby's house.

Franks forehead dipped low. "She's going to stay at your house tonight?"

"Yes. I know, it's strange, but I got peace about it."

"If you say so," slurred out from him. "I pray that everything works out. I'll keep my phone's volume on high in case you need to call me."

"I'm sure I'll be fine. But thank you anyway."

Seeing and hearing Frank's concern was only a preview of what I'd get if I told my oldest boy, Son, about Eunice staying with me. He'd probably come over and take fingerprints first. Between him and Frank, I wasn't sure which one was the most protective.

Me and Frank wasn't no kind of couple, but you know that's just something men do—they look out for the people they care about. *Real* men, anyway. I wasn't complainin'.

We was one of the first couples there that night. A little early. Instead of rushing inside, Frank turned off the engine, powered down our windows a few inches and sat. A cool fall breeze whisked through the car. Almost too cool.

I reached down and raised my window a bit.

"Sorry about that," Frank apologized.

"No problem."

Then he sat there for a minute, looking out the window. "Sure is a nice night out."

"Yes, siree."

Frank's car sits up high, so I got nosy and looked down into the person's car parked next to us. The front seat was clean enough, but the back seat might as well have been on that Hoarders TV show. *Lord, let me stop judging people.*

When I flipped my head back around, I was deadlocked with Frank. And there he was looking at me with those "goo-goo eyes" is what we used to call 'em.

"Wonder if Miss Gavina needs any help setting up," I declared while scrambling to find the latch so I could get out of the vehicle.

"Wait," Frank stopped me. "B, I need to talk to you about something."

All of a sudden, I felt claustrophobic. I rolled the window all the way down so I could get some air. *Oh Lord, what he want?* "Yes?"

Frank repositioned a little higher in his seat. "I don't know about you, but I really enjoy our time together."

"Me, too," I could honestly agree.

"And I've been thinking."

He waited so long to speak, I had to ask, "About what?"

"About me and you."

Chile, when Frank grabbed my hand on that armrest, I almost lost my breath.

He squared his eyes on mine. "B, I'd like to be more than your friend and dancing partner."

*Oh, Jesus. What do I say?* Me and the Lord hadn't had no kind of conversations about me and Frank being more than friends. *God, why didn't you warn me?*

Then, the Holy Spirit reminded me that I'd had some hints. Frank wanted to sign us up for next year's couples dance-a-thon. He'd brought up the idea of me attending his daughter's 40th birthday party. The thing was, every time I got a hint, I tucked it in the back of my mind, instead of talking to God about it. Now that it was time to have a discussion, I was at a loss for words.

"Frank, I don't quite know what to say."

He shrugged his shoulders. "I guess you could...say what you're thinking."

"Well, I'm thinking that…um…we got a good friendship going here and I'm fine with that. I thought you were okay with it, too."

He gave a conciliatory nod. "Yes, it is a good friendship. But being with you has reminded me that I miss close companionship. Affection. You know?"

Maybe last month I could have said I didn't know, but the truth was, I did. You watch a movie with somebody and you want to talk about it for the next couple of hours, but you can't when that person's already gone home and it ain't decent to call so late.

"I do understand what you're saying, Frank. I just…I don't know how to *do*…how to *be* more than friends with a man. I ain't never had no boyfriend-girlfriend relationship. You know, me and you come from a day when a girl got married and had her first real kiss all in the same day. We didn't have all this middle ground folk have today. Friends with insurance or whatever they call it."

"Now, B, come on. We *did* court back then," he countered, his eyes still gleaming at me. That Frank sure did clean up nicely.

"Yeah, but courtin' was a family affair. In my day, I courted right there on my parents' couch with my Momma in the kitchen, the next room over. And my little brother stuck his head in the room every five minutes."

Frank and I laughed at the idea. Times were different back then. Folk didn't do all this tryin' every Tom, Dick, and Harry on for size. When we courted, we couldn't give all ourselves to a man. Some folk say that was wrong because we didn't really know each other real private-like until we got married.

But I tell you one thing, when the right one *did* come along, we didn't have our heart all calloused up from so many rough relationships. It's better to go in fresh and naïve than bruised and carrying a whole lotta baggage, if you ask me.

Of course, me and Frank wasn't exactly fresh. Neither was the man asking me to marry him. Really, I didn't know *what* he was asking me. Fiddlesticks, I was too old to be playing games and trying to read minds. "What exactly is your definition of more than friends?"

His eyes rolled up into thinking position while I waited for his response. "I want…hmm…how can I put this? I want the opportunity for a closer relationship. If it doesn't work out, it doesn't work out. But I want the chance to…hold your hand."

*Okay.*

"Rest my arm on the back of your seat."

*Okay.*

"Kiss you goodnight."

*Now you done crossed the line.* "I was alright until you got to the last part."

"Kissing?"

"Yes, kissin'," I repeated. "All that kissin' and neckin' is too much. I can't agree to kiss nobody I wouldn't just as soon spend the rest of my life with. And I don't see myself signin' up no time soon for that route."

"I'm not asking you for a lifetime commitment. I…really, I don't know what I'm asking, B." He sighed in frustration. "All I know is I haven't felt this way about anybody in a long time and I thought this was what I was supposed to ask, but it looks as though I was wrong."

I chuckled. "Don't feel bad, Frank. Looks like neither one of us knows what we're doing."

"You can say that again." He laughed, too, and the worry wrinkles smoothed out of his forehead. "B, let's just go inside and dance before I make a fool of myself and make you even more uncomfortable."

"Now *that* I can agree with."

# Chapter 5

We both managed to put that awkward conversation aside and enjoy our night of dancing, followed by a light snack at the ice cream parlor. But I had to hurry up and get out of there before too long 'cause dairy don't always agree with my digestion.

Afterward, we made good on our plan to pick up Eunice from Libby's house. Frank was a little taken back, I could tell, at the sight of her. Them thigh-high shorts wasn't coverin' up none of the cellulite as he helped her hobble down the driveway to the car.

I stayed on the porch a bit longer to have a quick talk with Libby and see if there was anything she needed to warn me about. Sure enough, there was. "B, I got in touch with her son again. He said Eunice mostly lives at a first-come-first-serve shelter. She couldn't have gotten a bed tonight if she'd gone back that late.

"He also said she one of them free-spirit types. She don't like to follow no rules, got a problem with sustainin' relationships, which is why she homeless most of the time. Done busted out of a few senior citizen places and all. She been to and fro with counselors and therapists since her children's father died, but she ain't hardly changed none."

Made sense. "Is she on any medication?"

Libby shook her head. "She's supposed to be, for her circulation, but she probably don't take it. She ain't usually dangerous to anybody. Her son says it won't be long before she scats out again because she can't hardly stay with nobody."

I sighed, too tired to ask any more questions. "I'll call you in the morning and we'll go from there."

"Night."

Me, Frank, and Eunice rode on home. He helped her into the house and said goodnight to me the same way he always did—with a quick hug. "See you next Friday if the Lord says the same."

"And the creek don't rise," I added with a smile.

I almost had the door shut when he interrupted me. "B."

"Uh huh?"

"What about Sunday? Could we get together after church, maybe, and have lunch?"

I thought we'd left all that talk about being more than friends at the parking lot. But I could see Frank was still trying. "Not this Sunday. We got a Friends and Family program at three o'clock."

"Oh?" Frank's eyes lit up.

It took me a second to realize he was hoping I'd ask him to come, but he was too much of a gentleman to invite himself. So adorable. I batted my eyes a few times. "Dr. Frank Wilson, would you like to accompany me to the service Sunday afternoon?"

With a nod, he answered, "I would love to."

"Perfect. Be here at two forty-five, please."

"Will do. Night, B."

"Night."

I nearly jumped at the sight of Eunice standing within a foot of the door after I'd closed it.

"I'm sorry," she giggled. "That was sweet, though. He's madly in love with you."

I shook my head. For God's reasons, I felt free enough to share my thoughts with Eunice. "I can't say I totally agree, but I don't think I can *do* this whole falling in love thing."

Eunice glanced at the photos of Albert, our kids, and me on the wall. "How long you been widowed?"

"Eight years. Almost nine."

"Yeah, it's hard to move on. But you can do it. I buried two husbands. One from alcoholism, the other from cancer."

"Oh my," I gasped. Couldn't imagine going through such pain twice. Now that I was getting a close look at Eunice, she wasn't really as old as me and Libby. Must be the smoking, the extra weight and lowerin' two husbands in the grave had put fifteen years on her appearance. "I'm so sorry for your losses."

"Well, don't be. It was their time," Eunice resolved as she let her behind tip over onto my couch. Her feet came up off the ground momentarily as she flounced into place.

I decided to rest my dancing feet on the ottoman as well. "You get enough to eat at Libby and Peter's?"

"Yeah, but, you know, they don't cook like *we* do."

"Who don't?" I asked.

"You know. White people. Libby fixed a really bland turkey and some asparagus. All of it *grilled*, not a stitch of bacon grease or butter anywhere."

Chile, I had done forgot all about the differences in traditional black cookin' and white folks' cookin'. Miss Eunice was in for a big surprise if she thought I had some hamhocks and chittlins in the kitchen. After looking in my refrigerator and pantry, she might accuse me of being white, too. "Sounds like a mighty fine meal to me."

Eunice's hair flopped dramatically as she lowered her chin. "Are you serious?"

"Sure am. I eat more green stuff than anything else."

She took a deep breath, looked me up and down. "Well, looks like it's working for you. But I can't be on a strict diet. I can't be on a strict *anything*. I've got to live my life the way I want to. That's one thing losing my husbands taught me. Tomorrow's not promised to anyone. You've got to live every day like it could be your last. And if that stuff I ate at Libby's was my last supper, I can assure you, I am very disappointed."

The expression on Eunice's face was so funny— eyes bucked, lips puckered—I couldn't even get offended. I could see now how she won over people she'd never met. Maybe because she didn't have no hidden agenda, didn't pose no threat, people didn't have a reason *not* to open up to her.

"Well, when my great-grandson, Cameron, comes over, I do have to indulge him."

She looked around again. I assume taking in the grandfather clock, the china cabinet, the custom drapes and heirloom quality furniture, all the results of God's blessings set on Albert's hard work and good money-sense. "You live in this big house all by yourself?"

"Yep. Just me and Jesus."

"And you don't want a man like Dr. Wilson living here with you?"

I chewed the inside of my cheek, thinking about her question. "Naw. Can't say that I do. I guess if God says different, I'll take a husband. But other than that, nope."

She gave an exaggerated frown. "I don't blame you. Men have all kind of problems. They leave facial hair all over the sink." She held up one finger.

"Ooh, tell me about it," I raised my hand in agreement.

She shot up another finger. "They still think gross stuff is funny."

"You got that right, too."

"Now, I'm not trying to be vulgar, but my second husband used to fart so loud and hard, one time I thought somebody was knocking on the front door. And girl, I said, 'who is it?'"

Lord knows I don't normally sit up and talk about this kind of unlady-like stuff, but she sure was telling the truth.

"And don't get me started on the snoring." She threw her head back on the couch, gaped her mouth open and started honking through her mouth and nose like…well, like a man!

"Eunice, stop!" *Whoo!* My eyes got to waterin' from laughin' so hard.

"Graaaaaaw, uuuuuuuuh, graaaaaaw, uuuuuuuuuuh," she inhaled and exhaled.

"Girl, you need to quit!" I couldn't hardly see her no more for the tears, and my stomach had started aching, thanks to her perfect re-enactment.

Then she leaned over and began laughing at her act, too. Only her giggles led to a coughing spell she had some trouble coming out of.

"Eunice, you alright?"

"Water," she croaked.

I rushed to the kitchen, grabbed a bottled water from the ice box, and rushed back to her side.

She took a few swallows. "Mmm, thank you." Eunice coughed a few more times. "I haven't laughed like that in a very long time."

"I don't see why not. You're a comedian," I told her.

"No. I just call it like it is. Men give us plenty to joke about, if nothing else."

Eunice yawned, and I took that as my cue to lead her to the spare bedroom she'd be using. "You 'bout ready to retire for the night?"

"Yes, ma'am." Eunice rocked herself up from the couch and followed me down the side hallway to my daughters' old room.

Hadn't been too long since my granddaughter, Nikki, and my grandson had used that room to escape her deranged ex-boyfriend. And shortly after that, my nephew, Derrick, had stayed with me while he was on judge-ordered lockdown.

Now, I know the Lord would definitely have me open my doors to family members. But that night, as Eunice and I worked together to spread out the fresh sheets on Debra Kay's old bed, I had to listen and let the Spirit minister to me. See, it's easy to feel obligated to help your own flesh and blood. Even though Derrick was my nephew by marriage, he was still blood-kin to my late husband and my kids, so I expected myself to be there for him.

However, Eunice was different. She was quite literally off the streets. Even though she was only staying for the night, I knew this was a big step for God and me.

*Thank you, Lord, for giving me a heart to share Your love with people I don't even know.*

At the time, I didn't realize exactly how much love-showin' He had in store for me.

# Chapter 6

The Lord got me up extra early Saturday morning and took me through First Corinthians. Took a whole page of notes in my journal—some on division within the church, wisdom from His Spirit, the apostles, immorality in the church, marriage, food, freedom in Christ, love, and the gifts of the Spirit. His word is so rich!

Individually, the notes made sense, but taken together, it seemed like a hodgepodge. But I know He's purposeful in all His ways, 'specially when He's training up His children. I bowed my head and prayed in the Spirit for a while, but no extra revelation pertaining to those verses transferred into my mind. Instead, I found myself praying for Eunice and her son, whatever problems they got between the two of them.

I also felt led to pray for my pastor and for my fellow Mother's Board member Henrietta's continued healing following the diabetic coma. So far, her long-term memory was perfect, and her speech was almost back to normal. I laughed and told the Lord I wished He'd made her a little quieter, but I know He didn't really want a shy, soft-spoken Henrietta. That ain't the way He made her.

Still, I wasn't clear on what exactly He wanted me to meditate on or see in First Corinthians. So, I ended our quiet time with a prayer for my own understanding. "Lord, I know you gon' make it all clear to me, so I'm just gon' wait and see what You want me to hear from Your word. I know You are faithful to teach me, and I praise You in advance. In Jesus' name, Amen."

I checked in on Eunice. She was sprawled out on the bed like somebody who'd collapsed after spending fifteen hours working in an underground mine. I mean knocked O-U-T, out! If it hadn't been for her belly heaving up and down to show her breathin', I might have gotten worried.

Gently, I closed the door and thanked God again for allowing me and Libby to help Eunice. No telling when was the last time she spent a night in a bed, let alone a bed*room* all to herself.

I left her to sleep for a little while longer. Didn't have nothing on my agenda until noon. I could get to Libby's, to Mesquite, and back to Peasner within two hours, so there was no particular rush.

After all the time I'd spent in the Word, I really wasn't hungry. Praying first thing in the morning fills me up, but unless I'm fasting, I do make a practice of eating breakfast to get my metabolism going. That's one thing they taught me and Libby back when we met in the weight loss class: you got to keep your metabolism working like a big dog until a few hours before you to go to bed. Otherwise, it'll take off work early and leave everything you eat to turn into blubber.

Eunice had already made it clear she didn't like to eat healthy stuff. Normally, I wouldn't contribute to somebody's deathly habits, but since she was probably all healthed-out from Libby's cooking, and since she was only an overnight guest, I decided to whip up some old-fashioned pancakes. Just so happened, I had some real butter left over from when I made the 7-up cake for Cameron the previous weekend. (I thought he was gonna eat himself sick!)

I threw a little salt and pepper on some turkey bacon and left the yolks in the scrambled eggs. A little low-fat cheese topped off the eggs—with the right brand, nobody can tell the difference about cheese.

A few minutes after I'd finished all the cooking and rinsed off the last skillet, I heard Eunice's cane tapping up the hallway. She'd changed from the one-size-fits-all muu muu I let her borrow back into the clothes she'd been wearing the day before, fanny pack and all. "Morning, B."

"Back atcha."

"Smells so good in here, I thought I'd died and gone to heaven."

I chuckled, "Well, if heaven smells like bacon, my late husband is rejoicing right now."

I noticed how Eunice took a look at my Bible, then sat clear on the other side of the table, as if the Word might bite her.

"You hungry?"

"Most certainly," she squeaked.

Decided I'd sit on Eunice's end, keep her company. Soon as I set her plate down, she tore into it. Bless her heart, probably only used to eating pre-packaged, cold meals.

As usual, I said a blessing over my food and then took a bite of pancake.

"Just so you know, my mother taught me to pray over my food, too. I'm no heathen."

It tickles me when people who were brought up the right way as children apologize for strayin' from their home-training. Their conscience be confirming the promise of God. It's just a matter of time before they come back to their training, according to the Word. "You alright with me, Eunice."

She angled her forehead toward my study area. "I'm only saying, since I see you've been reading the Bible, now you're saying grace and all. I say grace in my heart. Thank God every day for my life and what little health I've got left."

"He is good," I affirmed the praise. "Do you get to church often?"

She shook her head emphatically, her jowls jiggling accordingly. "No way, Jose. I don't do church."

"Why not?"

"I like God and Jesus just fine, but I don't like rules."

"What kind of rules?"

"Can't do *this*, gotta do *that*. Can't wear *this*, talk like *that*," she griped, emphasizing her words with a swing of her fork. "But when you catch them breaking their own rules, they start preaching about forgiveness. Huh! Church is a farce."

Now, y'all know I *love* the church. Me and Albert donated the land for the church I attend to this very day. Next to Jesus and my family, the church is my heart. "Not every church is like that."

Eunice rolled her eyes. "Oh, please. You and I both know if I walked into any church right now wearing these shorts and this shirt, the people would stare me down."

I wouldn't say it out loud, but people were probably staring her down every place except the homeless shelter. Not too many women with her shape were brave enough to wear a fitted T-shirt anywhere, let alone a church. "That may be so, Eunice, but you can't throw out the baby with the bath water."

The corners of her mouth tightened. "B, you're a fun person. You've got your life and I've got mine. Let's leave it at that."

Seeing her struggle to rise to a standing position, I grabbed the empty plate from her hand so she could push herself up.

"Thank you."

"Sure thing. You 'bout ready to head to Mesquite?"

"I'm gonna take a smoke outside first before we leave, if that's alright with you."

"No problem."

Eunice helped herself to the front porch while I finished getting dressed for the day. I unfastened the rollers from my head, let my silvery gray curls fall, then swept them over to the side with a wide-tooth comb. At my age, I couldn't help but thank God I still had a head full of hair.

Next, I dusted my face with powder. A little ruige on my cheeks, eye brow pencil to fill in the rest of my arch. I picked a peachish-red lipstick and pressed my lips together to spread the color out.

I'd already laid my clothes out for the day. White eyelet blouse with a pair of denim pants, a little dressier than jeans but not too formal. Leopard-print ballet slippers added a little spunk to my attire. I took in my whole presentation in the full-length mirror handing on the inside of my closet.

*Not bad, sister.*

I reckon my gettin' ready took all of fifteen minutes. I still hadn't heard Eunice come back in the house, but since I have no earthly idea how long it takes to smoke a cigarette, I didn't get a notion to check on her for a bit longer.

Chile, by the time I went outside to see about Eunice, she was nowhere in sight.

"Eunice?" I called for her.

No answer.

"Eunice!"

My neighbor's dog barked in response.

I stepped off the porch and around to the side of the house. Then, I checked the other side. No Eunice. With hands on my hips, I stood in my front yard and took a whole three hundred and sixty degree turn. Still, no sign of her. "Lord Jesus, where did she go off to?"

Then my mind got a wild thought—did somebody kidnap her? Snatch her right off my porch? "Lord, protect her, in Jesus' name."

Unsure of whether I should call Libby or call 9-1-1, I swiveled to go back inside. That's when I noticed the greenback sticking out from under my flowerpot. I lifted the bright orange container and retrieved a fifty dollar bill. On it were three words written in blue ink: "Thank you, B."

# Chapter 7

I called Libby right away. She didn't seem too surprised. "I told you her son said she's basically a grownup runaway, B." Nonetheless, Libby promised to try and leave a message for Eunice's son so he'd know his mother was on the loose again.

I was glad to know Eunice hadn't been taken against her will, and I appreciated her token of gratitude, but the whole situation didn't sit right with me. I done seen people run away from a lot of things. A safe ride home with a caring person wasn't amongst the list of reasons.

The situation with Eunice bothered me so, I couldn't pay Ophelia and Henrietta no attention on the ride over to Hope Temple (which we now called our "sister church") for the fourth-Saturday women's fellowship.

"B, you alright back there?" Ophelia asked, eyeing me through the rearview mirror.

"I'm fine."

Henrietta countered, "Yeah, you quiet as a church rat."

Now, everybody knows the saying is church *mouse*, not rat. Sometimes, I couldn't tell if Henrietta was trying to make fun of me on the sly, or if she really was confused.

"Don't mind me none," I told them both.

Ophelia and Henrietta had done got closer since Henrietta had the stroke. Since they lived a few blocks away from each other, Ophelia had made it her ministry to tend to our sister when Henrietta's daughter couldn't.

"How your great-grandson doin'?" Henrietta asked.

"Oh, Cameron's fine. He should be over again in a few weeks."

Henrietta could switch subjects on you in a split second. "You know, my cousin's boy been in and out the hospital."

"Really?" Ophelia prompted her to continue.

"Yeah. They say he got autism of the mouth," Henrietta informed us with an authoritative nod.

Both me and Ophelia been around long enough to know that when somebody's mind is slippin', it don't do no good to try and correct 'em all the time. That just make 'em agitated. They already know something ain't right. No need in makin' the announcement.

The meeting with the women of Hope Temple would, hopefully and prayerfully, be one of legacies the Lord let me leave behind. Our church already had a Titus 2 wives' ministry going strong. While we were fellowshipping with the other ladies, we were also helping them get theirs started. One of their preachers, Rev. Dukes, had been the interim pastor at Mt. Zion while Pastor Phillips was tending to his wife during her last days on earth.

I had some issues with Rev. Dukes and his wife, Cynthia, at first. But the Lord saw fit for us to come to a resolution and work together. Ever since then, we'd had it on the agenda to join forces with the young and old at both our churches to try and teach the things women used to pass on in each other's homes, back before we all left our houses and started workin'.

I got nothin' against a woman having a job outside the home. But we all foolin' ourselves if we believe it ain't costin' us something.

"I hope they gon' listen to us good," Henrietta swapped the subject again. "I ain't got time to be wastin' on no hot-tailed, hard-headed young folk. My days short enough as it is." She started chewing on her bottom lip, rocking back and forth gently in the seat.

"Well, even if they don't, Henrietta, God knows your heart. He'll reward all we do in His name," Ophelia calmed her.

"Yeah," Henrietta agreed, "God got the record. And you know what? It sure was warm in my house last night."

"Is that right?" Ophelia kept with the flow. "What'd you have the temperature on?"

"I had it on twenty milligrams," Henrietta declared. "But you know, sometimes doctors don't know what they're talking about. I bet *his* house ain't warm at night."

"I know that's right," I could only agree. Inside, it made my heart sad to hear Henrietta's jumbled up thoughts. I had to keep praying for restoration, and keep thanking God that at least she could still walk and talk and go to the restroom all by herself. Some people can't even do *that* much.

As I helped Henrietta get out of the car, I noticed she was wearing a pair of thick black socks with white, dressy church shoes. I stole a glance at Ophelia. She shook her head and I knew right then this must have been something Henrietta insisted on. We both let it go.

Cynthia and the rest of the women in attendance from Hope Temple gave us all big hugs. Then, she opened up with in prayer and passed out the agendas. Our Titus 2 leaders, Janice Jamerson and LaTonya Wilcox, were first to share. They, along with two other women from Mt. Zion, had four tables set up in four corners of the fellowship hall. Then they led a speed-learning class. Kind of like speed-dating, they said.

Chile, I ain't never heard of no speed-dating, but if that's the way they meetin' up these days—spend a second saying 'hi' and then move on to the next one—no wonder folks havin' such a hard time stayin' married!

Anyway, there was one station for learning how to make a graham cracker crust, one for making natural cleaning products out of lemons and oils, one for twisting natural hair, and the last one for how to get stuff for almost free by matching coupons with the circular ads. In half an hour, the women from Mt. Zion had rotated all twenty or so of us through the four stations.

The ladies, young and old alike, wrote down all kinds of reminders using pen and paper as well as those tablets everybody carryin' around these days.

I had a few thoughts about letting my hair go natural. Well, *nappy* is what we would have called it back in my day. They shared some research about the connection between black women and how perms done caused an increase in all kind of womanly problems for us—endometriosis and the likes. Made me think twice about what I been slatherin' on my head, not to mention all my clients' heads during the years when I did hair part-time at the salon.

I wasn't ready to let go of my perm and pull out my hot comb just yet. Best thing for me to do would be have Son go on the internet and look up the research for me. When he got to sniffin' out something, he was like a hound dog.

My goodness, I was so godly proud of our women. Put a smile in my heart to see the ladies ministering to one another.

Truly, I'd forgotten they was expectin' one of us older mothers to share something as well, until Cynthia turned all eyes toward us. "We are so glad to have you mothers here. We're thankful for practical knowledge, of course. But we're even more grateful for the wisdom of more seasoned women of God. So, are you all going to share or will one speak today?"

By the way Ophelia and Henrietta looked at me with them blank faces, obviously they had forgotten, too. Or maybe we never knew? I don't know. Good thing the Lord reminded me of everything I had in my Bible bag.

"Well, one thing I can share is *how* I meet with the Lord every day," I started, pulling the contents of my bag onto the rectangular table. I had my Bible, a few highlighters, my journal, and a book on abiding in Christ, just so happen I was reading at the time. I put my cell phone on the table, too.

I held up the Bible first. "This here parallel Bible is my favorite one because it has two translations, New King James and Amplified. If I really, really don't understand something, I pulls out this iPhone and go to my Blueletter Bible app, then I can look it up in the original Hebrew or Greek and see exactly what all the words mean in the old way."

The younger women had all kinds of questions about how I studied the Bible. They wanted to know if I sang, what I sang, how I knew what to write in my journal, how I pray, how I kept track of my prayer requests.

Before I knew it, they was takin' notes on *my* notes. "Ladies, this is all sweet and flattering," I interjected, "but don't get all caught up in how me and God talk to one another. Everybody is different. God don't hardly do nothing exactly the same way with two different people."

The women was scribblin' fast as I talked. Finally, I shared the complementing book. "Sometimes, I read a portion of a book in my prayer closet. This one here by Andrew Murray. He one of the old South African saints. His work is real deep. You got to take in a little at a time."

"Is Mr. Murray in America now?" one of them wanted to know.

"No, honey, he with the Lord now."

They busted out laughing like I'd said something comical. "What?"

"You said it like he moved somewhere."

"He *did*," I stated. "Moved right on back home."

I suppose most people would have left it at that, but seem like the Holy Spirit pushed a pause button inside me and made me stop to process their response. The problem wasn't what I'd said—the problem was, the eternity God had in store for the saints wasn't as real to them as a place like California or New York. They lookin' at God's word like it's a "good idea," not like it's the truth.

*Speak through me, Holy Spirit.* In a split second, a passage I'd read earlier that morning popped in my head.

"Ladies, take out your Bibles if you have them. I wanna show you something. And I want you to let the Lord write this on your *heart*. Not your paper, not your mind, not your electrical doo-dad—your heart."

The enemy almost distracted me as I wondered how so many of them came into the house of the Lord without a Bible, but I had to remember where I was and what I'd come to do: teach them what they didn't know, not judge them.

They coupled and tripled up so everyone could look onto a Bible with someone.

"We all came here today to learn from one another. And the mini-sessions was great, done in excellence. Thank you so much, Janice and LaTonya, for sharing those practical things so we can honor God in everything we do."

The sisters gave them a round of applause before I carried on, "And you've asked the older ladies to share our wisdom. But I think the best wisdom I can share is where I *get* my wisdom from. Go to first Corinthians chapter two verse seven." While they turned, I gave them a little background on the book of first Corinthians and why Paul was writing this particular letter.

I started reading. "New King James, verses seven through nine. But we speak the wisdom of God in a mystery, the hidden wisdom which God ordained before the ages for our glory, which none of the rulers of this age knew; for had they known, they would not have crucified the Lord of glory. But it is written: Eye has not seen, nor ear heard, nor have entered into the heart of man the things which God has prepared to those who love Him."

Some of them had already heard that part about the eyes and the ears; I could tell by how they whispered it as I was reading.

"What these verses mean to y'all?"

Cynthia spoke first. "It means the things of God are hidden. No one knows what God has in store for His people."

A couple of 'em agreed with *mmmm-hmmm.*

Cynthia's right-hand friend, Karen, contributed to the conversation, "Paul was letting them know that God's mysteries are greater than what we can understand."

I let them spout all their understanding, which was basically the same thing over again, even from the ladies of Mt. Zion. Then I said, "Let's keep reading. Verse ten. But God has revealed them to us through His Spirit. For the Spirit searches all things, yes, the deep things of God. What does that tell ya?"

They got to squintin' and looking at that verse again. Then Karen cautiously whispered, "Is he saying that we *can* know the mysteries of God?"

"That's what it said, ain't it?" Henrietta snapped indignantly. "The word says what it says—even *I* know that."

"But," one of the younger ones asked, "people read verse nine like it's *spooky*, like we shouldn't even think God will tell us things. And so…are you saying God shows us secrets that He doesn't show everybody else?"

"Honey, it's not what *Mama B* sayin', it's what the *Bible* sayin'. Let's read it again—sometimes you got to read it more than once, you know?"

This time, I read all the way to verse sixteen, where the Bible says we have the mind of Christ. "And you know if we have His mind, there's nothing we need to know that He will hide from us. It's all in Him, and He's all in us."

They was sitting there like somebody just told them a rich uncle had died and left them ten million dollars. Only the wisdom of Christ is worth much more. Priceless

I had said enough. If I ever wanted them to hear the Holy Spirit speak for themselves, I had to trust Him to pick up right where He told me to leave off. *Write it in 'em, Holy Ghost. Thank You.*

I looked over at Ophelia and Henrietta. Ophelia winked at me. I winked back. Our work there was done.

The three of us rode back to Peasner in good spirits, even singing a few praises. Henrietta like the old hymns, and she got a voice that hit those notes just right. Make you remember the days when the saints used to sing with no organ, no drums. All we had was our voices, maybe a tambourine, and our hands to praise Him.

We'd just about made it home when I got a text from Frank: *Eunice admitted to hospital.*

# Chapter 8

Right away, I called Frank. "What happened to Eunice?"

"Looks as though she was trying to break in somewhere. She's got a fractured nose and several lacerations," he informed me.

"Break in *where*?"

"I'm not sure...a vacant house, maybe," he suggested. "As soon as they finish patching her up, she's going to jail."

I sighed. "Okay. I'll call Libby so she can get hold of Eunice's family. Hopefully they'll come see about her."

Tell you one thing, having a doctor friend working at the hospital was the next best thing to having a hotline to the emergency room. He kept an eye out. "Thank you, Frank, for letting me know."

"No problem."

I did my best to explain the situation to Ophelia, but I couldn't very well do so with Henrietta butting in every few seconds with topics having nothing pertaining to the conversation.

"Ophelia, I'll call you later," I finally said, hoping she would catch my drift.

"It ain't nice to keep secrets from somebody sitting right in the car with you, B," Henrietta scoffed.

Just when I thought I could skip one past her wits, she regained them. Funny thing how the mind works. "I'm not keepin' secrets, Henrietta. Nothin' for you to worry yourself about."

"Mmm hmmm," she settled.

After Ophelia dropped me off, I barely had time to set my bag down in the house before I U-turned right out the door again to pick up Libby. But instead of the hospital, we was on our way to the jail because Frank gave me the word they'd already transferred Eunice.

You know what? On the way to that jail, I started thinking to myself. *Why am I rippin' and runnin' all over town tryin' to help somebody I don't really know? How do stuff like this always end up on my plate?*

Really, I was just an elderly woman trying to live out my golden years in peace. Had my own house, my own life, and my own family to be concerned with. If Eunice's kids didn't want nothin' to do with her, nine times out of ten it probably had somethin' to do with the way she *didn't* raise them. Not tryin' to judge her, just saying it's always a serious reason behind a man who don't care about his Momma.

Anyhow, whatever happened between them wasn't my fault. Plus, I could have used a good nap after the women's fellowship. This business with Eunice had done messed up my sleep.

With my own well-being in mind, I declared, "Libby, if her son won't get involved, I think we ought to let the state step in. Only so much we can do, you know?"

"What you think the state's gon' do?" Libby wondered.

I shook my head. "I don't know, but I'm sure Eunice ain't the only senior citizen without a place to go. And they got plenty of our tax dollars to figure it out. We done paid our dues."

"Now, B, this don't even sound like you talkin'," she chided. "Since when do you pass folks on the side of the road so they can wait for the *real* Samaritan to come by?" Libby always got to remind me of the word—even when I don't want to listen at the moment.

"Eunice ain't exactly on the side of the road. She's in jail. Got three hot meals and a place to sleep. Might be safer for her in there, anyway. Least she won't be sneakin' off people's porches, worryin' 'em and such."

"Well, if you didn't care nothin' 'bout Eunice, you wouldn'ta worried about her so."

Surrender swept over my heart as I thought about Libby's words. Eunice was old and homeless. Coulda been me if it wasn't for the grace of God. One of the songs Henrietta sang earlier sprung up in my heart. *If it had not been for the Lord on my side, where would I be?* Right then, I knew exactly where I would have been – in Eunice's shoes.

*Thank You, Lord. I don't even want to think about where I'd be if You hadn't been with me all the days of my life.*

I didn't know what all the Lord had planned for me and Eunice, but somehow I knew before Libby even parked that Eunice would be coming back home with me.

Eunice's son sent the money to bail her out of jail. Once again, his position as judge had persuaded the powers-that-be in our small town to bend the rules. Took a little while longer, seeing as she was already wanted for the fine she hadn't paid, which her son also handled after they mentioned it to him.

He sent his money alright, but he never once made an effort to drive the little thirty or forty miles it would have taken him to see his mother. Well, maybe it's a good thing he didn't. Eunice looked pitiful. Her nose all bandaged and taped up, eyes swollen, forearms wrapped in gauze. Her lip was busted, too, but that part didn't look as bad.

When I finally got her inside, all Eunice wanted was her pain medication.

"You don't need to take your pills on an empty stomach," I warned her as I lifted her feet up on the bed and pushed them beneath the covers.

"I don't think I can eat. My entire face hurts," she moaned.

I insisted, "Let's try a little broth."

She was able to get down a few spoons full of soup with the pills. "Thank you."

Even though she wasn't much for chewing, she still had a little left in her to tell me about how she'd gotten hurt. "So many foreclosed properties these days. The houses just sit unoccupied. Every once in a while, I find a nice one that I wouldn't mind staying in for the night."

"Eunice, you can't just go breakin' in somebody's house!"

"It wasn't anybody's house, really. The bank had already put the papers on the front door, I made sure of it. And I wasn't trying to break the window. I was climbing in, but I lost my footing and everything came crashing down, including my face on the hard, tiled floor. It's a good thing the neighbors were nosy enough to have already called the police when they saw me open the window, otherwise I could have been on that floor for hours or days before I got the wherewithal to get out of there."

"Chile, God is certainly looking out for you," I marveled.

"I know," she agreed. "They say He looks out for babies and fools."

I shook my head sharply. "Don't call yourself a fool, Eunice. You get some rest now." I patted her leg and stood.

"Wh…where are you going?"

"Back to the living room."

"Whaaaaat are you going to do?" she slurred.

"I've got to get some food together for afternoon service tomorrow. Then I'll watch a little TV, read my Bible."

"Mmmm." Her eyelids slowly closed. "Okay."

Softly, I walked toward the door.

"B?" Eunice whispered.

"Yes?"

"Thank you. You're my angel."

I've been called a lot of things, but it always hits a spot in me when somebody calls me their angel. Even if they are all drugged up or in some desperate situation, it's nice to be the one Christ uses to bring relief.

"Bless God, Eunice. Bless *Him*."

# Chapter 9

Eunice slept the rest of the night and on into Sunday morning, which put me in a tight spot. My house rules don't allow no able-bodied person to stay home during church service. Thing was, Eunice wasn't exactly able-bodied, not considering she probably still needed her rest as the drugs wore off and the pain kicked in.

The bigger problem was leavin' her. Now, I'm kind and loving and all, but I didn't like the idea of havin' a stranger alone in my house, even if she was halfway knocked out on pain-killin' drugs.

My only other option, though, was to stay home with her and miss church, which certainly didn't set well with me.

"Lord, You stay with her and watch over this house," I prayed as I walked out my back door then headed through my yard toward the church. As I made my way, I had to laugh when the Holy Spirit asked me a question: *Who do you think has been watching over this house every time you leave?* "You're right, Lord. You *been* doin' this job already."

He so excellent in all His ways.

I worshipped without one single care about Eunice being alone in my house. "I give myself away, so you can use me," we all sang with our organist, Clive, and the praise team. Every time I sing that song, I have to swallow my selfishness. Otherwise, I'd be lying in church. *My house isn't even my own right now.*

The thought of Frank worshipping beside me later on in the afternoon skitted through my mind a few times. I wondered if he would like Mt. Zion. Our choir. My pastor. Really, I almost laughed at myself. Been so long since I worried about whether someone else liked the same thing I liked.

After Angela made the announcements and the children's choir sang, we had the offertory. One by one, the congregation passed by the mothers' row with envelopes, cash, and checks in hand. Had to be a good seventy-five people or so in attendance that particular Sunday, not including the choir and the pulpit.

Some wore their Sunday best, complete with stockings or with handkerchiefs in the suit pockets. And some of 'em look like they done came straight from the nightclub. Breasts hanging all out, pants sagging all down. We didn't have all these walks of life in the church before Rev. Dukes came along. He started that youth outreach program with the free hot dogs. Ever since, our church got a lot of off-color visitors.

But once I got past the fact of too much skin showing, I could only thank God for bringing them back to His house and pray away the offense the enemy was trying to bring me. Satan will do anything to get your mind off track at church.

Couldn't help but notice Geneva's empty seat to the left of the pulpit area. That's where all the ministers' wives sit, so the ministers can look down and see their wives supporting them whenever they preach.

The enemy tried to steal my attention again with the dance team—another one of Rev. Dukes' projects that stayed around. Chile, one of them praisers had a belly that would not stay put under her shirt. That gut came spilling over the top of the pants that was already too tight to begin with.

*Help us, Lord.* Now I'm sorry, but if was she gon' get up there next to the pulpit dancin', she would have to put on some kind of under-fabric or maybe wear a sash. I know peoples are doing their best to make everybody feel welcome and included, but if you a big girl, you got to take extra precaution when it come to stuff like this.

*I hope she don't wear that again.*

No sooner than I had the thought, the praise team leader, Queesha, invited everyone to come back and see them perform again at the Friends and Family service. *Oh, Lord.*

Ophelia led the prayer for the sick and shut-in. In my mind, I added Eunice's name to the list since I hadn't had time to get her name to Angela for the bulletin. What I did have time for, though, was to write Ophelia a note about the dance team situation. As the choir sang its final song, I tore a sheet from my journal and scribbled: We need to talk to Queesha about the dance team clothes real quick.

I folded the paper in half and gave it to Henrietta to my left as I whispered, "Pass this to Ophelia."

Henrietta's nostrils flared indignantly. She squinted at me and looked down her nose like a mean usher from back in the old Baptist church about to pop your head for chewing gum in the sanctuary. "Is this church business?"

"Since you asked, yes it is."

"Well, I'm a member of this church, too," Henrietta huffed, "and I got every right to read this here paper."

Before I could put an end to her shenanigans, Henrietta unfolded the note and read what I had done intended for Ophelia's eyes only. Not that I didn't want Henrietta to know, but I didn't want it spread all over the church, you see.

"You got some nerve," Henrietta breathed down on me. "Queesha is my grandbaby, and I won't let you discourage her from the work of the Lord." Henrietta tore up the note and stuffed the pieces deep down in her purse.

"You don't think that gal's shirt was too short?" I accosted Henrietta.

She rolled her eyes. "I didn't see nothin' but my granddaughter's wonderful choreography. Queesha's just as good as *your* granddaughter, you know?"

I couldn't do nothin' but turn my face back toward the choir. I let Henrietta have that one for free. Couldn't blame nobody but myself for forgetting she wasn't quite all there.

Pastor Phillips started his message off slow, thanking several of the brethren for helping him trim the church's hedges. He preached from Romans chapter six about being dead to sin. He said a few things I didn't agree with, but that's normal, I think. You ain't got to agree with every word come out of your pastor's mouth any more than you agree with everything come out of your husband's mouth or your supervisor's mouth. Long as it don't happen too often and they still got the right heart, just respect the position, pray for a better understanding for both of you, and go on.

I figure since he had to preach again at the three o'clock service, Pastor didn't get himself too revved up in the morning service. We let out half an hour early and I did manage to snag a second with Queesha on my way out the front door. Once Henrietta had done passed on outside, I locked elbows with Queesha and whispered, "I need to chat with you for just a second."

"Yes, ma'am."

We stood there together while the majority of the members passed by, waving their quick good-bye's seeing as we was about to come right back in a few hours. Once I saw I could talk to her without an audience, I said truthfully, "Sweetheart, you are doing a lovely job with the dance team."

"Thank you, Mama B," she beamed all thirty-two.

*Give me the words, Lord.* "And honey, I know you want to do everything in excellence before the Lord, right?"

"Yes, ma'am," she said as her face crinkled a bit. "Is everything okay? Was the song okay?"

"Oh yes, the song was fine." I took a deep breath. Though I done corrected folks in love plenty of times before, it still ain't easy. "But Queesha, one of the dancers need on something extra so her belly won't show while she's ministering before the congregation."

Queesha's chest deflated and she leaned in to me. "I know, Mama B, but I don't know how to tell her without her getting mad. And I don't want her to feel like she has to dress differently when we're all supposed to be uniform."

"She ain't got to dress different," I said. "She just got to dress in her real size or have some kind of safeguard so when her hands go up, we don't all get a flashin'. Now, I know you don't want to hurt her feelings, but if you plan on being a leader, you got to learn how to take correction and give it, too."

"Thank you so much for saying something to me," Queesha said, her words laced with grace. "If no one had mentioned this, I probably would have dismissed the thought from my mind."

"Oh no, chile. If the Spirit put a check in your heart about something, you don't overlook it, you hear?"

"Yes, ma'am."

*Thank You, Lord, for helping her receive this in love.*

"But how do I tell her?" Queesha begged to know.

Just then, Henrietta come barging up to us. She grabbed her granddaughter's hand and pulled her out of my grasp. "Come on, Queesha. You ain't got to listen to this foolishness."

"It's okay, Grandmomma, Mama B was—"

"Stickin' her nose where it don't belong," Henrietta poked her *own* nose into my conversation with Queesha. "Let's go."

Poor Queesha didn't know whether to follow her grandmother or stay by my side. "He'll give you the right thing to say," I said as I released her arm, not wanting to put no division between her and family.

I had to get my mind on finishing up my food contribution for the after-service fellowship anyway. I waltzed on out the sanctuary, saying good-bye to Pastor on my way.

"See you in a few hours, B," he prompted.

"Oh, you know I'll be here with bells on."

Just then, Henrietta called my name like I was somebody's child outside after dark.

I stopped and turned back toward the church, putting one hand over my brow to shield from the sunlight. "What?"

Henrietta crossed her arms on her chest. "Who's that lady smokin' a cigarette on your back porch? And why she got all kind of toilet paper on her face?"

Lord, she said it so loud everybody left in the parking strained to get a good look at Eunice sitting in my lawn chair, huffin'-and-a-puffin' like a choo-choo train despite the bandages covering half her face.

I lowered my voice, walking back toward Henrietta in hopes that Eunice wouldn't be offended by all this. "That's not toilet paper, it's medical dressing. Her nose is broken. She's a lady I met at the food pantry."

Henrietta looked past my shoulder, I guess checkin' Eunice out. "She sure is fat. Don't look like she need no free food and no more pets."

"*Pets*?"

"You know what I'm saying. Don't try and change the subject," Henrietta growled.

I was speechless.

Henrietta carried on, "And for the record, don't be tryin' to tell my granddaughter what to do when you livin' with cigarette-ment in your own house!"

Pastor approached us, his right hand raised in a gesture of peace. "Sisters, is everything okay?"

The last few stragglers went ahead and got in their cars, thank the Lord.

"Yes, Pastor, everything is fine," I stated as calmly as possible. *I can't let Henrietta get to me.*

"No, it ain't." Henrietta pointed toward my yard. "She got somebody over there smokin' a cigarette."

Pastor's eyes followed the finger to Eunice, who waved back at us between drags.

"Pastor, she's a homeless woman. She fell and hurt herself yesterday. I'm housing her until we can figure something out."

"And she's smokin' cigarettes!" Henrietta insisted he acknowledge.

"Yes, I see. B, you keep up the good work," Pastor commended me.

"Good work? How she doin' good work while she got the devil stayin' with her? And tryin' to tell my granddaughter what to do?"

Pastor gently cupped Henrietta's elbow. "Now, sister, who are we to judge?"

Henrietta smiled and softened her voice. "I guess you're right, Pastor." Obviously, she was pleased that she'd gotten the Pastor's attention enough to warrant his touch.

He turned and led Henrietta to her car, then he winked at me. I took this as my cue to escape.

I knew Henrietta was sick. I knew she was delusional. When peoples are off their rocker, we all got to be patient with them.

But that don't always stop your feelings from gettin' hurt.

# Chapter 10

Eunice smashed the butt of her cigarette on my concrete and then nearly fell trying to bend over and pick it up so she could dispose of it properly. Maybe I should have felt sorry for her, but I ain't never had no ashtrays around, and I didn't plan on startin'.

"How was church?" she asked as she followed me into the house with a limp.

"Just fine," I smarted off.

"Well, pardon me for asking," she said.

I shook my head, trying to erase all that foolishness with Henrietta out of my brain so I could keep good manners toward my houseguest. "I'm sorry, Eunice. That woman who was pointing over here at you...oh, never mind."

"Yeah. I could tell she wasn't too happy about me being on your porch, for some reason," she chuckled.

Her laughter helped me to calm back down to myself. "Can you help me out in the kitchen?"

"Surely. I was going to finish up the potato salad, but I know better than to mess around in another woman's kitchen. That's one sure way to lose a friendship."

Even though I didn't agree all the way with her philosophy, I was a little glad to hear her call me friend. Considerin' the fact that she didn't really have nobody to call on in need, my guess was she didn't have many friends. And after the way Henrietta had treated me, look like I was down to just two friends, myself—Libby and Ophelia. Not that me and Henrietta ever saw eye-to-eye, but I knew she would never leave me out on the streets.

Despite Eunice's arms being all bandaged up, she was a help in the kitchen. She got busy spooning the chocolate chip cookie dough on the metal cookie sheets while I finished the redskin potato salad.

"You sure are cooking quite a bit, here. Are you expecting company?"

"Oh, no. Well, yes. Company at the church, not here. We've got friends and family day at the church this afternoon," I informed her, thankful for the chance to invite her to my other home.

"That's nice," she said real quick-like.

We were both working on the counter space on either side of the sink. She didn't bother to look at me any more once I mentioned church.

*Help me, Holy Spirit.* "I'd love for you to come to the service."

"Now, B, I already told you, I don't do church."

"I see," I said. Not missing a beat, I requested, "Retch me a fork out from the drawer."

Eunice took a step back so she could open my utensil drawer. "Here you go."

"Thank you. Mind if I ask why you don't do church?"

"I was raised in the church. My mother made us go every major holiday," she bragged. "Every time we went, she gave us a dollar to put in the offering plate. Still, the people looked at us as though we were Martians who'd dropped out of the sky. Scary."

Me and Eunice musta had two different ideas about what it means to be raised in the church. Raised in the church, to me, mean goin' to service at least three times a week—more than that before desegregation. Not to mention choir rehearsals and other business meetings.

But she was right about one thing: Church folk sure do look visitors up and down when they come in the building. We ain't never meant no harm by it. Don't you look at people you ain't never met? I, for one, ain't never considered myself a stranger in *any* house of God. But I see how we could make somebody feel funny comin' to church with all our starin'.

"I'm sorry you felt that way," I apologized on behalf of the all churches everywhere. "But if you get there early, like I do, people don't get to look at you so hard. They might not even notice you."

"Another thing," Eunice added, dumping the last spoonful of dough onto the second cookie sheet, "what's with all the money stuff?"

"Money stuff?"

"You know." She twirled her spoon in the air. "Give ten percent, give to the building fund, give offering? It's no wonder church people are always the poorest ones in the bunch. I think if God wanted some of my money, He'd just give me less."

"Giving is always up to you," I came back at her. "The Bible says give with a cheerful heart. If you don't have a heart to give, you shouldn't do it. But don't let that be the reason you stay away from church. God would much rather have *you* in church than your money any day."

"Maybe God would, but I'm sure the pastor wouldn't."

*Hmph.* I know a rebellious spirit when I hear it. I ought to – I used to have one. Didn't want nobody tellin' me what to do, least of all my husband, even though I knew he was only lookin' out for the good of our family.

But one day, I overheard myself telling my youngest child, Otha, "If you would just do what I tell you, things would work out so much better." And no sooner than I said it, the Holy Spirit whispered in my heart: *That's what I've been tryin' to tell you, B.*

From then on, He give me a check in my heart to let me know when I'm actin' up. I don't always listen, but at least I can't say I didn't know.

I'm still prayin' for Otha. Look like I was gonna have to pray for Eunice for this, too. "When you get to know Jesus, you do what He asks you to do because He lives in you. You love bein' who you are in Him. He's better than the old you."

"No disrespect to Jesus, but I like me and I don't want to change. I'd like to end this particular discussion, if it's all right with you. I don't like to talk politics, religion, or child-rearing. It's a no-win conversation because everybody already thinks they're right." She dunked the empty bowl into the hot, soapy water in the sink.

Normally, I would have had a come-back for Eunice. I would have tried to convince her that I understood church ain't all perfect, but it also ain't all bad. But inside me, I heard a familiar phrase: *Be quiet.* Of all the stuff the Holy Spirit tell me, this usually be the hardest one to obey.

I put the final touches on the potato salad, then hung my apron on the nail right beside my refrigerator. "I'm gonna lay down for a spell before the afternoon service. Can you take the cookies out in ten minutes?"

"Sure thing. And don't mind me," Eunice said. "I'll be taking another pain pill in a bit. That'll put me out for quite some time."

I didn't like the sound of that. "You hurtin' a lot?"

"With a broken nose and thirty-seven stitches, anyone would be."

The bruises beneath her eyes were certainly the kind that looked worse before they got better. I happened to look down at her legs and noticed that the bad one appeared to be swollen and a little darker color than the good one. "Your leg okay?"

"Aaaah," she scoffed, "it gives me a little more trouble every once in a while."

I figured she knew her own body, so I left it alone. Sure enough, by the time I got up again for church, Eunice was fast asleep.

# Chapter 11

I changed into a black maxi dress with a silver belt and a flower print jacket. These young folk tickle me thinking they really doin' something new with the flower print fabric we wore in the 60s and the 80s. Sometime, I put on something older than *them* and they say I'm in style.

Frank showed up at two forty-five dressed in a gray Miami Vice lookin' linen suit with a green shirt and a multi-color paisley tie. I know it don't sound like a fashionable outfit, but Frank pulled it off well. Probably too well. Even though I looked good for my age (if I do say so myself) him wearin' that suit made it seem like we had more than seven years difference between us.

"B, beautiful as usual," he said, barely crossing the threshold into my house. He stood with both hands behind his back.

"Come on in," I waved for him to follow me. "I need your help getting some things over to the church."

"My pleasure."

Frank and I packaged up all the food and headed out the back door. Lord knows, I really hadn't thought that one all the way through because the very first person my eyes met after I locked the screen behind me was Henrietta. She took a step out of her car and got an eyeful of me and Frank coming out of my house.

Even from a far distance, I could see the shocked expression on her face. I sped up to get in front of him and run interference.

Every one of Frank's steps made two steps for me, so I had to do double-time to get ahead, but I had no choice. No telling what Henrietta might say to him if I didn't threaten her with the shut-up eye first.

Me and Frank walked past her without incident, thanks to her picking up on my body language. Really, though, Henrietta was not the first one who didn't know how to take Frank. "Oh, Mama B, I didn't know you had a *friend*," and "Where you been hidin' him?" and "You been' holdin' out on us, Mama B," they remarked between winks.

I suppose they all found me and Frank quite comical, but I didn't, this being the very church my deceased husband built and I was coming into my second home with another man. And then I wondered where Frank was gonna sit. He wasn't on the Mother's Board. And he couldn't sit with the deacons, like Albert used to. *Why didn't I think of this earlier?*

All those nervous feelings attacked my stomach, just the same as they did when I first went out with Frank. *Lord, help me.*

Me and Frank made it through all the little observations of my church family and took the side door into the sanctuary. Thank God, the seat behind where I normally sit was open. At least I'd be in the same area, and we wouldn't be shoulder-to-shoulder with Henrietta.

I'd never been so happy for Clive to start playing than I was that day. Finally, all eyes switched from me and Frank to the choir as they marched through the main doors. Maybe they weren't *all* watching us, but it sure felt like it. I had some empathy for Eunice now.

The choir sang one of our old-time favorites, "Do Not Pass Me By." Lord knows I wasn't tryin' to measure Frank's church-goin' experience, but after Eunice gave me a new definition of what it means to grow up in church, I needed to test and see if Frank had some kind of church background. Otherwise, we might have a mismatch of understandings.

I snuck a peek at his lips to see if he actually knew the words. "Hear. My. Hum. Ble-cryyyyyyyyy," the choir sang. To my relief, Frank's lips moved in unison with the rest of us. *Thank You, Lord.*

By the third song, the church was close to packed. Every time I turned around to see the crowd, I noticed another face I hadn't seen in years. I certainly didn't want to bring attention to myself, but when people waved, I had to wave back or blow them a kiss. So nice to be around people you know and love and worked alongside in the Lord's Kingdom.

Angela gave the welcome, followed by a response from one of the members of the St. Luke Baptist. Ophelia read the occasion and introduced Rev. Dukes as the MC. Then, to my surprise, Pastor took the pulpit.

"I was glad when they said unto me, let us go into the house of the Lord," he started, to which the church replied with an agreeing 'amen.'

"To the Mount Peasner church and to our friends and family, again, I want to publicly thank all of you who have been so gracious to me in my time of bereavement. I received so many cards, so many encouraging notes, so many offers and shows of help from so many of you since my lovely wife, Geneva, passed away. Again, I want to say thanks."

"Mmmm hmmm," from all of us.

"I also see the good Dr. Wilson present today." Pastor gestured toward us. "Thank you for taking such good care of my wife in her last days."

Frank nodded.

Pastor cleared his throat. "But there's one thing I've learned in all this, and that is to give flowers while they can be smelled," he continued.

"Amen."

"Once a person is gone, you won't have the chance to thank them."

"You right," Henrietta barked.

"Now, I know we've never done this at Mt. Zion Baptist Church, but I have to tell you that when I called around to make several personal invitations to the Friends and Family Day program, so many people asked about one person in particular that I knew beyond the shadow of a doubt we needed to honor this long-time member."

Immediately, I started thinking about Ophelia. She's always helping with the programs and stepping in when people back out for whatever reason. And she do so much stuff that people don't even know about, like how she been so good at taking care of Henrietta. I could hardly wait for Ophelia to get her moment in the spotlight!

Pastor said, "She has meant so much to the church. Literally, she and her husband donated the land we worship on today."

*Goodness, he's talking about me!* My heart got to skippin' so fast.

"And so today, we want to take some time to honor a faithful member of Mt. Zion Baptist Church of Peasner, TX. Mother Beatrice Mama B Jackson, also known as Mama B."

Folks got to clappin' and standin' while they was lookin' my way. Frank stood up, too, and smiled at me. Then he held out his hand to help me up, and Lord knows I needed his help because my knees was a-shakin'. *Me?*

A flood of love washed through my heart and came spilling out of my eyes. I grabbed Frank's hand and held onto it in plain confusion. In fact, I dragged him all the way to the end of our row before I realized I'd been holding onto him.

Clive started playing the graduation song as I joined Pastor on the level below the pulpit. That Clive can be so silly sometimes, but I love him, too.

LaTonya from the wives' ministry placed a bouquet of flowers in the crook of my elbow while Angela gave me a gift bag to occupy my other hand. And Pastor read off a letter from the city of Peasner decreeing the following Monday to be Beatrice "Mama B" Jackson day.

Y'all, I know there's more to what happened when they honored me, but I was so shocked by it all, I don't remember half of it. I just remember I could hardly see the whole thing from all the tears in my eyes.

All those hands clappin', all those people hollerin' for me. People coming up to the podium saying 'thank you' for helping me raise my daughter, for saving my marriage, for bringing me food, for praying with me, for the card I sent, for the money I gave—most of that stuff was done in secret. It was, I hope, a preview of what it will be like to hear Jesus say, "Well done my good and faithful servant."

I know it will mean more when He says it, but it was nice to hear on earth.

After all the hoopla, I returned to my seat. Frank set my gift basket on the floor and winked at me. That little wink was awful sweet.

But soon as I settled back down, Henrietta turned her head around and hissed, "You ought to be ashamed of yourself, acceptin' that award when you know you shackin' with this here doctor. As if you ain't rich enough already. Shameful."

She whipped her head back before I could respond.

Frank must have heard her accusation. He gave me a quizzical stare. I shook my head in response. "I'll talk to you later."

We managed to make it through the rest of the reunion service without incident from Henrietta. I did my very best to steer clear of her path. When we all moved to the fellowship hall for dinner, I waited behind, talking to people, so Henrietta could be far away from me.

Of course, in the process of staying behind to chat, everyone wanted to meet Frank. A few people already knew him from his work at the hospital, but most of them were just impressed with the fact of him being a doctor.

Sister Inez, who always got some kind of ailment, took the liberty of rolling up her sleeve and showing him a big, nasty boil on her elbow. I mean, that thing look like the devil himself tacked it onto her. "Whatchu think I oughtta do, Doctor?"

"I think you need to go to your doctor," Frank advised.

"Uh hun," she said, "that's exactly what I told my husband, but he don't think nothing's wrong with me. I'mma tell him I got a *professional* opinion. Thank you."

"You're welcome."

We finally made it to the kitchen. Pastor made room for me and Frank at his table, right alongside the Dukes's and Rev. Martin. We ate, talked, and laughed so much that I forgot about being all jittery with Frank around my church family. Truth be told, I had been worried about how people would receive Frank, seeing as so many of them adored my husband. But they actually seemed to kind of like the idea of me and Dr. Wilson. I had gotten my nerves all worked up for nothing.

The younger ladies forbade me to help them in the kitchen. Shooed me slamp out the way. "We got this, Mama B. You go on and entertain your male *friend* over there."

By this point, I figured I might as well go on and get over their teasin'. I snapped my fingers. "I most certainly will, thank you very much." Couldn't help but laugh at myself.

"Woooh!" Janice cooed. "Go on, then! If anybody deserves to be happy in love, it's you."

I waved off her words and returned to the table wondering, *Is that what they think? I'm in love?*

Most of the peoples was gone out the fellowship hall by then. Our table was clear except for Cynthia, seeing as the other menfolk had excused themselves and gone back to the business office for something or another. One of Frank's old buddies pulled him outside to catch up.

I figured I'd stay inside until they finished washing the empty containers so I could retrieve mine. I love the church folk, but I don't trust nobody to return my good Pyrex bowls after a potluck.

Now that it was just me and Cynthia sitting at the table, I noticed a certain coolness about her. Come to think of it, she really hadn't had too much to say to me. She'd talked around me, but not to me. *Must be something on her mind.* "Cynthia, sweetie, you alright?"

She blinked, picking at something on her skirt. I followed her hand motions and saw that there was absolutely nothing wrong with her skirt.

"Seem like something's bothering you."

She took a deep breath. "Mama B, I really don't know if I should say this."

I felt my forehead crinkling up as I witnessed the troubled expression on her face. "Well, if you don't know, I won't press you." If it's one thing I hope I done taught women, it's to keep your mouth shut until God give you the words.

But she blurted out, "It's…Dr. Wilson."

She had done let the cat out the bag, now. "Oh? What about Frank?"

"Just…be careful with him. He hasn't always been the kind, thoughtful, *faithful* man he's presented himself as today. Leopards don't change their spots."

Woman-to-woman, I knew what she was hintin' at.

Pastor, Rev. Dukes, and Rev. Martin mozied on back in the fellowship hall just then. In a way, I was glad because I didn't want to encourage Cynthia to keep talkin'. On the other hand, I wanted to know the details. How exactly did she know Frank? How exactly did she know about his faithfulness, or lack of it?

Well, if I was anywhere close to hopping on the "in love" train with Dr. Frank Wilson, I had reason to check my ticket twice now.

# Chapter 12

I tossed and turned so until I had to get up out the bed that night. *Frank? Unfaithful?* Now, I know everybody got a past. Everybody got something they gon' take to the grave with 'em. But Cynthia had started me on thinkin' about Frank's moral character.

I knew about the wine-drinkin' and the cussin'-movie watchin', but those were things I realized I would have to leave between him and the Lord. Albert did plenty of stuff I didn't think was right, but I didn't really know about 'em 'til after we was married. Good thing, too. Back before the Lord changed me, I didn't know how to stay in love with somebody who wasn't doin' what I wanted them to do.

Had to be about one o'clock in the morning when I got up to use the restroom. I called myself being quiet so I wouldn't wake Eunice, but she was up. The light shined under her door, and I heard her mumbling to somebody must be on the phone. Couldn't make out the words, but she wasn't havin' no friendly conversation, that was for sure. Sound like me *and* her both was havin' a rough night.

I took something for my lactose intolerance and then ate a cup of yogurt with fruit and granola. Albert used to laugh at me 'cause even my midnight-munchies snacks be healthy.

On my pass back through to my bedroom, I wasn't trying to eavesdrop on Eunice, but her voice came through clearly. "How many times do I have to apologize to you? Don't you know it's haunted me every day for the past fifteen years?"

*Goodness, no wonder she's so miserable.* Been punishing herself. I didn't know who was on the other end of that line, but it musta been somebody important for her to be up arguin' with them at that time of night.

Suddenly, I heard Eunice's phone slam shut. She began to weep softly, yet loud enough for me to hear it on the other side of the door. I stopped. Put my hand on the doorknob, wondering if I should try and go in or leave her to the Lord and her feelings. Since I wasn't sure, I rapped on the door to ask her.

"Eunice, you okay?"

"Um...yes. I'm so sorry I woke you."

"It's all right. I was already up gettin' a snack," I spoke to her through the door.

I heard her sniff. "A snack sure sounds good right about now."

Gently, I cracked the door open and peeked in with a smile. "I've got some yogurt."

"No offense, B, but yogurt is *not* comfort food." She tapped on over to meet and follow me back down the hallway with her cane in hand. "Have you got anything sweet or crunchy?"

We stopped at the pantry. I took a look inside, with Eunice directly behind me.

"You've got popcorn," she spied, pointing to the top shelf. "That'll do."

I stretched to retrieve the box. Had to check the expiration date to see if it was still good. "This must be your day. It's still okay, but it's the healthy kind. No salt and no fat."

"We could pour butter and salt on it," she suggested.

She just determined to eat all wild, I see. I figured I might as well share my secret stash with her. "I've got some butter and cheese sprinkles I put on my great-grandson's popcorn when he's here."

As the popcorn popped in the microwave, I watched Eunice fidget at the table. Seem like she was itching to get something off her chest. Lord knows after Cynthia's big bombshell, I wasn't in the mood for no more confessions.

The timer went off. I fixed her bowl Cameron-style, smothering the white puffs until it looked more yellow than white. Have to admit, it smelled so good, I took a napkin and trickled some onto a napkin for myself. Not too many.

Eunice crunched and closed her eyes in bliss. "Mmmmm. This is so good. Thank you."

"You're welcome."

"I used to make popcorn for my kids. You remember those popcorn poppers where you had to pour the kernels into a well and the popcorn came shooting out of the yellow top?" She smiled.

"Yeah, we had one of those. Did you ever do the kind where you put the tin pan over the stove's eye?"

Eunice threw her head back in laughter. "Oh my goodness! I almost burned up our house with that one!"

I was glad to hear her talk about some good times with her family. Warms a mother's heart. "How many kids?"

"Three. One died in an accident. Got two left. The judge and the teacher. Not too bad, huh?"

"Not bad at all," I complimented her. "Sounds like they've done good for themselves."

"What about your kids?" she wanted to know.

Chile, we got to talkin' 'bout our kids, their degrees, and their jobs. Then we went down memory lane, talkin' 'bout all the times they broke stuff in the house, the crazy pets they had, and their silly jokes.

Turns out, Eunice's deceased son died in a car wreck when he was a teenager. Drunk driving accident. By the Spirit, I knew this had something to do with why she'd been upset for the last fifteen years. Since I ain't never lost a child, I don't know that pain. I don't know what kind of mess it would have made me if I'd gone through such a loss. And lost two husbands, too? *Lord, have mercy.*

We stayed up bumpin' our gums until almost two o'clock in the morning, and y'all *know* I don't be out the bed after 9:00 p.m. unless the Lord say otherwise. But that Eunice was a lot of fun to talk to. She made me remember what it was like to come home and unwind with somebody.

Albert could talk your ear off! Sometimes, he'd be talking so until I fell asleep on him. That didn't hardly stop him, though. He'd shake me and say, "B, you up?"

I'd yawn, "I am now." Ha!

Eunice finally said, "Ooh, I'm 'bout to hit the sack."

"Me too."

"Thanks for listening, B."

I squeezed her hand. "Thanks for letting me listen."

Eunice rinsed out the bowl and set it in the dishwasher. We turned out the kitchen light and returned toward the bedrooms. "Night, B."

"Night."

When I got back in my room, it hit me that I hadn't said one word to her about the Lord. I didn't feel bad about it, though. Eunice the type don't respond to somebody preachin' about love. She the kind that got to *feel* it before she'll listen to words.

Me and Eunice made a trip to the Walmart and got some more groceries for the house. Of course, folk was starin' at her with all that riff-raff on her face. Her eyes weren't so bad anymore, but since she had taken the bandages off her arms, anyone who got close could see the black string sewn into her skin.

She rode around in the handicapped buggy, throwing all kinds of foolishness into the basket. Good thing we had already decided she should be well enough by the end of the week to move back to wherever she wanted to go. In the meanwhile, she said she needed some "real" food.

That Eunice was something else. I didn't have a scale to prove it, but I know I'd put on a few pounds already, bein' in her company. She had cut loose in the kitchen a few times and managed to put enough seasoning and honey just right on a chicken breast—make you wanna holla! I had a mind to let her cook as often as she wanted to after that.

She grabbed a few pairs of pull-on pants, shirts, and a pair of flip-flops.

"It'll be getting cool soon. You might want to get something a little warmer," I suggested.

"Yeah, you're right. Some of those shelters might as well be made out of paper for as cold as they get in the winter," she said, dropping a sweatshirt into our stash.

I, personally, wasn't looking forward to dropping her off at some shelter, but I could see she was getting antsy. She was smokin' outside more. Mumbling to herself. She wouldn't agree to go to the upcoming Wednesday night service. She apologized, said I didn't have to worry about her breaking my rules much longer.

"B, go on and get what you want," Eunice prompted several times as we swept up and down the store's center aisles.

"We ain't at the fruit and vegetable section yet. That's where I do most of my grocery shoppin'," I said.

"Well, whatever you want, just throw it in the basket. I'm buying," she insisted.

Put together, our bill came to a little over eighty dollars. Then she added cigarettes and that took it up to a hundred. She pulled out a VISA card, swiped through the machine. Of course, I didn't pay no attention to what all she was doing as she conducted the transaction.

But when she was done, the girl gave her cash. Eunice thrust it into my hand before I knew what she was doing. "Here you go, B."

"Eunice, I ain't asked you for no money."

"I know. I'm *giving* it to you."

The cashier chimed in, "Shoot, I'll take it if you don't want it."

Well, I'm not one to insult someone who's trying to bless me. I stuffed the money into my pocketbook. "Thank you, Eunice."

Since Eunice had to walk to the car on her cane, of course she trailed behind me. Good thing, too, 'cause now I was starting to wonder where Eunice gettin' all this money from.

I got to doin' the math up in my head. She said she gave the person who brought her to Peasner fifty dollars, she gave me fifty dollars, she done spent a hundred dollars at Walmart and another hundred-and-something she had just gave me. That's goin' on four hundred dollars in less than a week, with no job to speak of. But she beggin' for food from the food pantry and stayin' in homeless shelters.

At the rate she was goin', she didn't need to follow nobody's rules. She could afford to get her own place and take care of herself.

Somethin' wasn't addin' up.

Eunice wasn't much help putting all the groceries away back at the house. Said her leg was botherin' her. Since she'd been wearing some pants that Libby brought her, I hadn't had an opportunity to see what was going on with her. But when I went in to check on her before I took my afternoon nap, I had to keep my composure. Her bad leg had done turned dark brown and was weeping from the pores.

"Eunice, you got to get to a doctor," I warned softly, trying not to scare her too bad.

"It's only cellulitis. Flares up from time to time."

"Has it been this bad before?"

She shrugged. "Can't say that it has. But everything gets worse as we get older, right? I'm guessing with the fall and the drugs and all, it might be taking a little longer to get better."

I shook my head. "This ain't healthy. I got a good mind to take you to emergency right now."

"You will do no such thing," Eunice protested, covering that leg with the bed covers, as though her condition would leave my mind if I couldn't see it any more. "I've seen enough doctors this week to last me the rest of the year."

"What about your stitches? And your nose?"

"The doctor said the stitches would dissolve on their own. And once a broken nose is set, all you need to do is let it heal. I'll take off the face bandages tomorrow."

She 'bout stubborn as my momma was. Couldn't get her to go see a doctor 'til it was too late. "Eunice, need I remind you, you ain't got no medical degree, far as I know. You got no business doctorin' on yourself."

She raised an eyebrow. "When you spend several years married to an abusive alcoholic, you learn to be your own doctor after a while."

Eunice grabbed the medicine bottle and half-full glass of water on the night stand. She popped another pill. "I'll be fine, B. You worry too much."

She could set up there and act like her leg was fine all she wanted to, but I knew better. Eunice was sicker than she thought.

# Chapter 13

Frank wanted to go for a light dinner after our dancing Friday night. I figure since I been up with Eunice 'til two in the morning, I could extend a similar courtesy to Frank. All those calories we burned on the floor would make up for eating so late.

Frank picked a steakhouse off of the highway. One I hadn't ever been to, actually, so I had to study the menu. So many new places popping up near Peasner.

"What'll it be?" he asked when I closed the booklet.

"Believe I'll have the chicken Caesar."

"Sounds good."

The waitress came and took our order, leaving us in a familiar spot across from each other. I don't know what it was about the lighting in that place, but Frank looked awful handsome despite his laid-back clothes. Bald head, brown eyes, smooth skin, shining white dentures. I could see why women might have thrown themselves at him, making a man's temptations even harder to bear.

All through our chit-chat as we ordered and waited for our food, I told myself to stop thinking about what Cynthia had said. Whatever Frank done in his past ought to stay there, like they say about Vegas. Still, there was a part of me that wanted to know. *What if Frank is some kind of womanizer? What if he makes a fool of me? It would be all my fault because Cynthia did warn me.*

I tried to take everything into account. In the past months, Frank had been nothing but kind to me. Sent flowers, took me dancing, let me take everything as slow as I needed to.

But he did make a habit of texting me before we talked. *Maybe he had to get where he could talk, get away from another woman? Maybe the reason his daughter stopped volunteering at the shelter was because he didn't want her to see me.* Then the enemy got real busy with the accusations. *What if his wife didn't die of a disease – maybe he poisoned her?*

Well, I'd had about enough of giving the devil room in my brain. If I was gonna be in some kind of a more-than-friendship with Frank—*IF*—I certainly needed to feel like I could be honest with him. "Frank. There's…something I want to ask you."

He swallowed and set his fork on the plate. "Yes?"

Had to discern how to approach this one. Can't very well come out and ask a man if he ever cheated on his deceased wife. "You remember Cynthia, from church the other day? She ate with us at Pastor's table."

"Oh yes," his eyes sparkled with remembrance. "The reverend's wife."

"Mmm hmm," I confirmed. "Well, she said something to me…something about you and…it bothered me."

He sat back, bewildered. "I didn't know I was so popular. What did she say?"

"It's not so much what she said. She hinted that…you had some issues in the past with…faithfulness."

The smile slipped from Frank's face. His eyes dropped.

Immediately, I knew I had hurt my friend. My heart hurt *for* him. I reached across the table and squeezed his hand. "Frank, I'm sorry. I probably shouldn't have brought it up. It's he-said-she-said anyway." *How could I have been so silly?*

He took a deep breath and yanked his gaze back to me. "No, no. It's okay. I'm sure Cynthia was only trying to protect you, and I'm glad you're comfortable enough to ask me hard questions."

Thank God he felt that way because I sure wanted an answer.

He inhaled. Exhaled again. "Cynthia was correct. There was a period of five years or so, right after I turned fifty, when I thought I was *the man*. Thought I was God's gift to black women all over the metroplex. It's amazing that I don't run into more relatives or acquaintances of the women I used."

*My Lord!*

"I was smart, had a prestigious career, made good money. Nobody said 'no' to me, except my wife. I was too stupid to know she was only trying to keep me grounded. I thought she was my enemy."

Sounded familiar. Plenty good men done fell into that trap.

"But then Margie began to suffer with Lupus and I realized I could lose the best thing that ever happened to me. None of those women meant what she did. It was like…like that moment when a big flash comes and you hear angels singing *Hallelujah! Hallelujah!* Like the Lord presented her to me all over again."

I smiled at the love Frank obviously had for his wife. I was also grinnin' because I liked the way Frank didn't get all huffy and defensive.

And he didn't give me one of them beatin'-around-the-bush lines a lot of men give when you ask how they treated their first wife—"I made some mistakes" or "I wasn't a perfect husband." The fact that Frank came at me straightforward said more about the character of the man sitting across from me than anything else.

"Did your wife know about the other women?"

"Yes. She found out. It took counseling, some nights on the couch, she threw a few dishes at me...but she took me back. She *actually* took me back. For the first time, I understood the love of Christ. Through her. Through reconciliation. I never forgot that I had the love of a woman I didn't deserve. Kept me at her side until her last breath."

Chile, I was 'bout to start cryin'. "She was a wonderful woman of God."

"She sure was. You would have loved her," he nodded with his own eyes watering. "You two have the same sweetness of His Spirit about you."

"That's 'cause *He's* sweet, you know?"

"Amen and amen."

The waiter brought our salads but apologized for leaving our garlic rolls. "I'll bring them right back."

My first thought was to tell him to leave mine since I don't eat much bread. But then I thought about Eunice. She'd walk a mile on that bad leg for a hot, buttery garlic roll. "Can you wrap mine up so I can take it with me?"

"Yes, ma'am."

Frank extended his arms across the table for prayer. We caught hands and he led us. "Father, thank You for being the great lover of our souls. Thank You for Your Son, Jesus.

"And thank You so much for bringing B into my life. I pray that You would glorify Yourself in this friendship. Teach us and keep us by Your Spirit. And now we bless the food we are about to receive. Thank You for it. Let it nourish our physical bodies as You continue to nourish our souls. In Jesus' name, Amen."

I whispered, "Amen."

Y'all not gon' believe this. For real. But the second my eyelids parted and looked at Frank again, seem like the scales fell from *my* eyes. I don't know exactly how God did it, but He opened up a window from heaven and shined some kind of special light on Frank Wilson before me.

I just about heard them angels singin' to me, too: *Hallelujah! Hallelujah!*

# Chapter 14

I stayed on cloud nine the rest of the dinner, gazing into his eyes, hanging on every word that flowed from his lips. Frank was smart. And *funny*!

He told me about patients with crazy problems, his first surgery, his first lawsuit. Apparently, the malpractice insurance for doctors almost made him quit.

I think our waiter got mad at us because we was takin' up the table so long, costin' him tips. But whatever Frank wrote on that receipt made the young man very happy, so I didn't feel so bad when we walked out at nearly a quarter 'til eleven.

Franked started the car, and I started a conversation I hadn't imagined I would have before the lightswitch for Frank flipped on in my heart. "What do you think we should do for Thanksgiving next month?"

He took his hand off the gearshift and stared at me. "Thanksgiving?"

"Yes. I'd love to spend Thanksgiving with you, seein' as it looks like we takin' things a little further."

All thirty-two of them…teeth come pointing at me. "B, you've made me a happy man tonight."

"Right back atcha, Frank."

Now, I done watched a whole lotta movies and read a whole lotta books and I knew what was supposed to happen next in these days and times. We was supposed to lean across the armrest and kiss.

Not saying I didn't want to kiss, but I didn't want to be forward. And Frank was too nice to make the first move, given what I had done already told him about neckin' and all.

But I was at a point where I knew I couldn't keep over-analyzin' everything. Couldn't keep comparin' Frank to Albert, comparin' 1975 to the twenty-first century.

Seem like I could almost hear Ophelia sayin', 'B, If you want to kiss the man, kiss him.'

So I hauled off and did it. Pushed my body right toward his, he met me halfway and I smacked him dead on his big lips. *Shucky now!*

Soon as it was over, I hopped back on my side of the car like I done somethin' I wasn't meanin' to do, except I did. And I was glad I did. Frank got his nice lips. Soft. And they covered mine completely. For some reason, that made me all jumpy inside.

"Woman, I didn't think I'd ever get any sugar from you," Frank teased.

"Me, either," I snickered. I touched my lips with my fingers, savoring the tingle he'd left behind. Still couldn't believe I'd actually done it. *What would*...no, I wouldn't even let myself wonder. For all we knew, Albert and Margie could be holding hands and sitting at Christ's feet having a praise party that very moment, not studyin' us at all.

The delight on Frank's face spoke all the way home, even though he didn't have a whole lot of words to say. He played a Smokie Norful CD, a nice mix of old and new songs. When he parked in my driveway, I asked Frank again about Thanksgiving.

"Oh, I'm sorry. I forgot all about it after you tackled me."

I gasped. "Frank Wilson, I did not *tackle* you!"

He grabbed my hand and kissed the brown side. "Don't worry. I won't tell anyone."

I yanked my hand from him and set my back against the door, doin' my best to give him the mean-eye, but it didn't work. We both started laughing at me. At him. At the whole situation.

"B, we'd better pray," Frank prompted.

"Wonderful."

Again, Frank asked the Lord to lead us, guide us, and be glorified in our friendship. He thanked God for both of us being far enough along in our healing to appreciate the new thing He was doing. He thanked God for His perfect timing and asked that He would give us hearts to always honor Him, in Jesus' name.

"Amen," we said together.

While Frank parlayed around to my side of the car, I grabbed the bag with Eunice's bread from the back seat. Though I would enjoy surprising her with the treat, a part of me felt bad for contributing to whatever health problems she already had, 'cause how she eat got somethin' to do with all her problems, I was sure.

As Frank escorted me to front door, I got a notion to ask him about Eunice's leg. After all he said about the malpractice, I wasn't quite sure he was at liberty to give medical advice off the clock. And I certainly didn't want him to think Eunice or I was trying to take advantage of his medical expertise. Just that I couldn't think of no other way to get Eunice help.

"Frank, Eunice done took off all her bandages and she seems to be fine as far as her arms and nose are concerned. But her leg's been givin' her a lot more trouble since she fell.

"I went in the other day and saw it's all dark and drainin'. I told her she should go see a doctor, but she won't listen. You think I ought to call 9-1-1?"

He raised both eyebrows. "If she won't go, she won't go. You can't make her. If it's not a life-or-death situation, the paramedics won't transport her unwillingly."

"Okay." My hands wrung themselves.

Frank relented. "I could look at her leg, if you want me to. If she'll let me."

"I don't want to put you in harm's way, professionally," I made myself clear.

"Looking won't jeopardize anything."

"Thank you so much," I said as I unlocked the front door quickly, before he could change his mind.

Frank followed me toward the bedrooms. I knocked on Eunice's door. "Eunice?"

"Yeah?"

"Honey, I've got Dr. Wilson with me."

"It's about time," she belted out. "Y'all go on. You won't bother me."

Too embarrassed to look at Frank, I kept my face toward the door. "He says he can look at your leg if you'd like."

The bedsprings creaked. "If it'll make you feel better, he can come in. But I'm telling you both upfront, I'm not going to any hospital."

I opened the door. Eunice lay on the bed wearing another one of my muu-muu's. She'd exposed her leg for Frank to examine. He switched on the lamp so he could get a better look.

"What's that you got there in the bag?" Eunice asked me, oblivious to Frank.

"It's garlic bread. It came with my meal, but I didn't want it so I saved it for you. You want me to warm it up?"

"You know I do," she cracked a silly-lookin' grin.

"First things first, you need to keep it elevated." Frank had switched into doctor mode, so I figured that was the proper time to get the bread heated up.

I stopped off at my bedroom and kicked my shoes into the room. Them dancing shoes are comfortable enough, but sometimes my feet swell after being up and out so long. And if you don't listen to nothin' else on your body, you gotta listen to your feet 'cause they won't hush until you give them what they want.

I set the bread on a plate and warmed it up for Eunice, then tip-toed on down the hallway so I could hear if Eunice was telling Frank some health information that she hadn't shared with me. Frank had already told me that whatever a patient tells him in confidence, he can't reveal without written permission. He was already puttin' his behind on the line for me. I figured if the time came for me to make Eunice go to the hospital, I wanted to be able to tell them what they needed to know without bothering Frank.

But, chile, I wasn't ready for the earful I got when I snuck up to the door.

"If B's too slow for you, I'm ready and willing," she mumbled softly. "And I can *make* myself able for somebody like you."

*Oh my Lord!* My chest pounded. *Did she just proposition him?*

Frank's voice came through, full of confusion. "Are you—"

"It's whatever you want it to be, good doctor," she made a second pass at him.

I slid back to the kitchen, hardly able to believe what I'd just heard.

"B, you got that bread ready?" Frank hollered loud and clear.

"Just about," I yelled back, trying to train my face real quick.

I stomped back down the hallway and set the plate on the nightstand. "Here you go, Eunice."

"Thank you soooo much, B."

Something in me wished I had some kind of powdered poison to put on that bread.

Frank stood at the doorway. "She definitely needs to get to a doctor as soon as possible. Looks like poor circulation, probably coupled with an infection. This could get in your bloodstream if you're not careful. But don't take my word on it—get it from whomever you see. This is all off the record. If they ask me anything, I'll deny I ever saw your leg."

"Yes, off the record," Eunice repeated, her eyes fixed on Frank's. "And I'll deny it, too."

I walked Frank to the door. He dusted my cheek with a kiss I barely even felt, thanks to Miss Eunice. He might have been trying to talk to me for a second longer, but I politely kicked him on out the door. "I'll see you…I don't know when."

"How about you coming to church with me Sunday?"

"Yeah," I agreed without even thinking. "That's fine. We'll talk tomorrow. Good night."

I paced back and forth across the living room. *How dare she? After all I've done for her!*

I wondered if maybe I should have confronted her with Frank in the room. Naw, I didn't need Frank there. This kind of thing is best handled woman-to-woman.

My first mind said to go back in that room, snatch my good 500-thread-count sheets off her body and order her to leave my house that very hour! She had some nerve layin' up in *my* bed, breathin' *my* heated air, makin' passes at *my*…man-friend. And callin' me *slow*, too!

My head throbbed with anger. *That back-bitin' floozy!* "Lord, Jesus!" flew out of my mouth.

"B, you alright?" the witch's voice called to me.

"Yeah!"

"Okay. This bread sure is good. Thanks for thinking of me."

"Uh hun." I was *thinkin'* about her alright. Thinkin' about how good it would feel to pack up all her stuff in them plastic grocery bags and set her right out there on my porch, then wake up in the morning to find her disappeared. This time I would *not* go lookin' for her. Just let her rot wherever she wound up, I didn't care. *I didn't deserve this! No wonder nobody in her family fools with her!*

The Voice of wisdom, which thankfully never sleeps or slumbers, came to the forefront of my mind. *B. Calm down.*

I managed to plant my behind on the couch despite my heartbeat springing all over the room. My hands, by virtue of all the years I've been walkin' with the Lord, I guess, formed a steeple at my forehead. "Lord, this is ridiculous and You know it. She can't stay here, Father God. She got to G-O, go."

*B. Calm down.*

I slammed my fists on my knees. I didn't *want* to calm down. You do something nice for a person— take 'em into your house, feed 'em, bring a *doctor* to see 'em, give 'em everything you have. And this is how they treat you? "This ain't fair, God."

*Jesus feels the same way.*

Now why He always gotta bring Jesus into everything, I don't know. Well, yes I do. I can be mad as I want to, but when I think about all He done for me, everything else happen be small compared to His goodness.

This little reflection was enough to bring me back to myself. I had to think this through. If I went in there and kicked her out, she would be, literally, on the streets with no place to go. Probably try to squat somewhere and bust her nose again. Not that it would be my fault, just that she'd be hurt when she could have been safe here in my home at least until daylight, when she could hustle her bad leg on back to wherever she wanted to go. Me kicking her out that night would be two wrongs.

Plus, there was the issue of her health. She couldn't have made it all the way down the street if she'd wanted to.

I grabbed my cell phone off the coffee table and sent Libby a text message I hoped she'd see first thing in the morning. *Give me Eunice's son's number.* This boy needed to come get his Momma quick, fast, and in a hurry.

When I finally settled into bed to process my heart with the Lord, my anger gave way to the fact that I was hurt. I certainly wasn't starvin' for friends, but…I liked Eunice. I thought we were going to at least be the kind of friends who'd catch up with each other by phone once or twice a year.

In seventy-two years, I done had my fair share of folk lyin' on me, gossipin', repeatin' stuff I thought was confidential, and undercuttin' me. I used to work in a salon, remember?

This was different, though. I'd never actually witnessed with my own ears somebody bein' so deliberately two-faced with me—for no *real* reason. *What Eunice gon' do with a man? She can barely stand up!*

I thought about all the times we'd sat up talkin' and laughin'. She'd cooked for me, told me I should be proud of my kids. Come to think of it, she'd given me the courage to move on past Albert. And she was one of the captains of the B-and-Frank cheerleading squad, next to Libby!

"Lord, how could she do me like this?"

*Jesus knows.*

He also wept. Which is exactly what I did, too.

# Chapter 15

Eunice's leg got to hurtin' so the next morning, she couldn't even get out of bed. "Call the doctor and tell him to refill my pain prescription," she begged me.

To be fair, I sat on the edge of the bed and tried to contact the doctor. His answering service said he wouldn't pick up his messages until later in the afternoon. They advised me that Eunice should take over-the-counter medicines until Monday or either go to the hospital.

Of course, Eunice didn't receive that news well. Oh, she moaned and groaned and writhed in pain, saying doctors were nothing but "overpaid nerds."

*She wasn't sayin' that when she hit on Frank.* "Lord, forgive me," I whispered under my breath.

"Forgive you for what?"

I guess I'd spoken too loudly. "Never mind." Since she was obviously in a lot of pain, I knew it wasn't the right moment to confront her about what she done the night previous. No, I wanted her undivided attention whenever we had that conversation.

"I got some ibuprofen in my room."

"No, I can't take that. It upsets my stomach. You got some Tylenol?"

"Sure don't." I was very glad to disappoint her.

*Stop it, B.* "But I'll run to the pharmacy to get you some Tylenol."

Her eyes glistened as she wiped her nose. "Thank God!"

*Yes, she'd better thank Him because left up to me, she'd be at a shelter.*

"I've got money in the front pocket of my fanny pack."

Since she'd offered, I reached into her stash and pulled out a twenty-dollar bill. Under any other circumstances, I wouldn't have dreamed of taking money from someone in agony. But I reckoned paying for her own medicine was the least Eunice could do.

Libby finally called me while I was at the pharmacy. "What took you so long?" I quipped.

"I told you we had the women's prayer breakfast this morning. Why? What's the problem?"

"Eunice."

"She run away again?"

"I wish."

Libby slurred sympathetically, "What happened?"

"Put it this way, when she said she shouldn't be in the house with Peter, she was right. And that's all I'm gon' say about the matter," I shut my trap.

"Well, I don't want to lead you into gossip and slander, 'specially since I just came out the church-house, so I'll leave it there, too. Here's her son's number."

I stopped to get a scrap of paper from my purse and jotted down the digits. "Thank you. I'll have to talk to you later. For now, be prayin' for her. That leg is really achin' her this morning."

"Will do. Bye."

Well, at least I'd put Libby in Eunice's spiritual corner. Lord knows Eunice needed somebody rootin' for her 'cause I sure didn't have an unction to.

The sign above the aisle led me to the row with pain relievers. Reluctantly, I grabbed the box of Tylenol off the shelf. Tramping back toward the counter, I heard a familiar voice call my name.

There was Pastor Phillips to my left, near the freezer. Instantly, my frown gave way to a smile. "Hello, Pastor!"

"Hi, B. Fancy seeing you here!" Glare from the overhead lights made his forehead shine even more. A healthy glow, I figured. Good to see him lookin' like ninety-five percent of himself again.

"Same to you."

"I didn't get to talk to you much the other day. How's your family?" he inquired.

"Oh, everybody's fine. Looking forward to a good Thanksgiving. I got four kids but don't hardly get to see 'em 'til the end of the year. Shame, you know? We got to do better."

He agreed. "And how's your friend—the smokin' one?"

I chortled. "Oh, she's 'bout as good as you can be after all she's been through."

"Yes. No matter how bad things are, they could always be worse."

I tried to think of what might be worse than a person bitin' the hand that feeds them. "Pastor, I gotta ask you a question." I scooted in closer to his basket.

"Sure, B. Anything."

My Pastor meant it, I know. He and I done had plenty counseling sessions. He a good shepherd, and Geneva was a worthy helpmate. She always added extra wisdom to his advice. I probably would have been done contacted Pastor about Eunice if I'd had that team in my back pocket. Now, Pastor would have to suffice by himself.

"You ever tried to be nothing but nice to someone, but they try to hurt you?"

He closed his eyes and nodded as though he already understood what I was trying to say. "Yes, B. I know what you mean. I've been praying for you ever since I saw that hint of contempt in your eyes toward Henrietta."

"Contempt?" *Henrietta?*

"Yes. I know it's hard to love somebody who doesn't treat you the way you deserve to be treated," he persisted. "But Jesus said in Luke six, if we only love those who love us and if we only do good to those we know will do good to us back, we're no different from sinners. Anybody can love somebody who treats 'em right. But a Christian has the power to love the people we know won't or can't return it to us. *That's* the love of Christ."

My lips stammered for the words to respond. For one thing, I wasn't talkin' about Henrietta. For another, why he use a harsh word like 'contempt'? Is that what I showed toward Henrietta? All I could say was, "Thank you, Pastor," 'cause he has surely bamboozled me there.

"I know you can do it. You've got the love of God in you. He will prevail," Pastor edified me.

Again, I expressed my gratitude. Me and Lord would have to get back to this little sermon later 'cause it flew straight over my head at the pharmacy.

I stole a look into Pastor's basket. Two microwave meals and a bottle of Sprite. "What you doin' eatin' all this mess? I thought the ladies packed some of the leftover food for you to freeze and eat this week."

"Yes," he looked away, "most of what was left was...you know...the stuff the peoples didn't want. For good reason."

"I see," I conceded. Basically, he was sayin' all they had left was Henrietta's food. "Not to worry, Pastor. Either me or Ophelia will drop by and bring you something later on."

"Yes," Pastor purred, "Ophelia. How is she?"

"She's good."

"Mmm. You know, the other day, when you brought Dr. Wilson to church...you got me to thinking." A shyness skidded across his face. "We ain't gettin' no younger."

"You right about that," I could only agree.

"I've been thinking about Ophelia."

"Yeah, I think about her, too. Maybe the Lord'll send her somebody soon. She's sure ready for some company," I spilled all her beans as I remembered her pressing me to acknowledge Frank's interest in me.

Pastor coughed. "I was thinking maybe...me and Ophelia..." he shrugged.

I narrowed my eyes as his clues sunk in. "You sweet on Ophelia?"

He rubbed his chin and shifted his weight nervously from one foot to the other.

Inside, I got so tickled. Me and Pastor was in the same boat. He ain't asked no woman out in so long, hadn't courted in so long, the only tricks he had up his sleeve was the ones he'd used back when he was young and insecure, in his early twenties; he was poking around a woman's friend to get a clue.

I had to help him out. "Why don't you call her and ask her to a movie?"

"You, um, yes," he stumbled. "Okay."

"Yes. Call her. I'm sure she'd be happy to receive the invitation from you," I encouraged him. Then I put a hand on his shoulder. "It's hard gettin' back in the swing of things, Pastor, but if the Lord has opened your heart to find another helpmate, that means He's still got work for you to do, and He knows you're going to need someone behind you."

His eyes shined. "I receive that in faith."

# Chapter 16

I really wasn't sure how that whole thing with Henrietta got brought into what I was saying to Pastor. In my mind, I replayed what happened when Henrietta accused me of harboring sin in my home. I thought I'd done a pretty good job of ignoring her.

I didn't have too much to say to her at the Friends and Family Day. She said something to me, of course, but I'd ignored those words, too, 'cause I know she ain't all there. Bottom line with me and Henrietta, I didn't have no feelings toward her. For the time being, I didn't see nothin' wrong with it. You can't make nobody act right, you know?

Pertaining to Eunice, I still didn't have no good idea of how to act with Eunice. *Lord, exactly how am I supposed to handle a snake?*

Like I imagined an addict must look while waiting for somebody to cut up the drugs, Eunice sat up impatiently as I opened the box of Tylenol. I squeezed and turned the bottle, poked in the protective foil, and pulled out the cotton ball. I poured two into her waiting hand.

"Give me another one."

Her request went against the label's advice, but in light of the fact she was a grown woman who'd probably taken more medication than most in her lifetime, I obeyed.

She downed the pills with the water I'd brought her. "Ummm. I hope this works," she whimpered. Sounded almost like a dog.

Suddenly, I remembered the time Son's dog, Blackie, nearly lost an inch of his tail after following my child into the house despite Son's orders for the dog to stay outside. The screen door slammed just before Blackie made it all the way inside, causing a nasty cut.

Of course, Son fussed at him for not being obedient. But I remembered telling Son to be nice to the dog. Blackie knew better than to come inside, he just didn't want to listen that time.

Son had fussed at Blackie. Told him, "That's what you get for being such a *bad* dog!"

I intervened at that point, rubbing Blackie's neck the way he always liked. "Don't be so rough with him right now, Son, he's hurtin'. Show him some mercy, even if it is all his fault," I had said.

That's when the Spirit watered and bloomed the seed Pastor had planted at the pharmacy: How could I show more love toward a dog than a human being? I wasn't supposed to be just toleratin' Eunice and Henrietta. I was supposed to *love* them. There's a big difference between the two.

I nearly choked at the revelation.

"B, you alright?"

Wasn't no doubt in my mind then about how to treat this trial the Lord had done placed in my life to perfect His love in me. I reached out and pulled her into a big hug. "God loves you, Eunice."

"My word, do I look like I'm about to die or something?" she babbled into my ear.

"No. I'm just saying, He loves you no matter what."

"Okay. If you say so."

I settled back on my bottom and looked her in the eyes. "*He* says so. And I love you, too."

Eunice's head tilted slowly as she blinked several times. "Thank you. No one has said that to me in a long, long while."

"Then it's about time," I said, propping her leg up on a pillow. "Let me pray for your leg."

She dropped her head and closed her eyes, and I took the liberty of asking God to heal her leg as well as open her heart to more love than she's ever known in Him.


I don't usually answer my phone when an unknown number comes across my screen, but seeing as it was Saturday, I figured the telemarketers were off duty. "Hello?"

"This is Paul Lemon. I got your message. How can I help you, Mrs. Jackson?" He said it all professional, like I hadn't told him my reason for calling was his own mother.

I went out of my way to sound friendly. "Yes, Mr. Lemon, how are you?"

"I'm fine, ma'am. How can I help you?" he repeated.

Goin' off the fact of Paul having manners (him calling me ma'am and all) I knew I needed to play the sweet old lady card. "Son, your mother's in a real bind here in Peasner. She hurt herself real bad—"

"Is she okay?" he cut me off, with a smidgen of genuine sincerity in his tone.

*Thank you, Lord.* "Yes. For now. But that leg of hers needs to be looked at and she won't go to a doctor." I tucked myself into a corner of the kitchen to be sure that, even if I had to raise my voice, Eunice wouldn't hear me.

"Trust me. Once the pain gets great enough, she'll go. She always does."

He had a point. A person can be as stubborn as they want to, but a sharp twinge *will* change a mind; have 'em beggin' for a doctor, a nurse, an aide—anybody with access to a needle.

It hurts to see somebody get to that point, though. "Well, now, I know you don't know me, sweetie, but...I'm a friend of your mother's."

He interrupted with a laughing cough. "She has *friends*?"

"Yes. I am her friend insomuch as I'm *for* her good."

He stopped his sarcastic clucking. "I see, ma'am."

"In addition to being her friend, I'm also a mother. And I know it would mean a lot to any mother for their child to come see about 'em when they down and out," I coaxed with a few intentional cracks in my voice.

"Not likely," he grunted.

"You mind if I ask why not, young man?"

"Umm," he mumbled, "no disrespect, Mrs. Jackson, but I haven't seen my mother in quite some time. She gets in trouble, she gets out of trouble. She makes friends, she burns her bridges, she moves on to her next victim...that's how my mother is. My sister and I stopped trying to change her a long time ago."

I could almost taste the bitterness in his words. My heart melted for him, for the fact of not having a mother for whatever reason. But the presence of anger meant he still cared. The boy in him hadn't given up on his mother, no matter what his grown-up lips said.

"That's fair, Paul. For what it's worth, your mother hasn't always been the greatest friend to me. I'm sure, whatever she did, she hurt you far worse than she hurt me, but she's still your mother and you only get one from the Lord. Now, you already got the right idea about not changing her. All you need to do from this point on is forgive her for not being the mother she should have been and accept her for the woman she is now—*imperfect* as she is because she needs you, son. She really does."

I heard him swallow hard. "I…even if I wanted to, it would be very hard for me to get to Peasner. I'm physically disabled."

"My goodness, and yet you still makin' it to work every day though, right?" I cornered him.

"Uh…yes, ma'am."

Had him right where I wanted him. "Well, bless God. My address is forty-two thirty-seven Miller Street. When should we expect you?"

His voice twittled around for a few seconds, but my immediate, silent prayer made it to God's heart before the enemy could feed Eunice's son another excuse. He exhaled loudly. "Tomorrow afternoon, I guess."

"Two-thirty will be perfect. I'll be callin' to make sure you don't get lost, all right, love?" I confirmed with my best southern senior citizen accent.

"Yes, ma'am."

"Alrighty then."

*Lord, forgive me for workin' that old lady "game" as Nikki would say.* Me and Him both laughed at me. It wasn't no game, really, 'cause I *am* old in age. We gotta have some kind of benefits.

I felt a press to get busy prayin' before this boy came over. I didn't know what Eunice did wrong, but I knew she did something right by raisin' him to give respect where it's due. Really, if more parents did just *that* much, we'd solve half the problems in the schools and put ten thousand prison guards out of a job.

Anyhow, I sent Frank a text and told him to pray for Eunice and her son. Of course, he called me back as soon as he got a break, wanting to know if there was anything he could do to help.

"No. Just pray. They got something going on between them. He's coming to see her tomorrow to try to talk some sense into her about that leg."

"Okay. Let's agree now. Father, we come to You asking for intervention between Eunice and her son. God, you know the healing that needs to take place between them emotionally, and you know what physical healing Eunice needs. God, I thank you for B's heart toward them. For the love that flows from You through her to people. Strengthen her as she continues to intercede. In Jesus' name we pray, Amen."

"Amen," I breathed again. Lord, that man sure could pray. I'm sure everybody on the Spirit-line got a jolt on that one. "Thank you."

"Everything will work out for His glory," he decreed.

Nothing else to say except, "It is so."

Me and the Lord talked for quite some time about the situation with Eunice and her son. I prayed that the Lord would mend Paul's heart and soften the bad memories of his mother.

I believe the Lord can move on a person's heart even if they're not a believer. He did it with Pharaoh, no reason why he couldn't do it on Paul, especially since all souls belong to Him anyway.

I prayed in the Spirit, too, because I didn't know quite what else to pray. When I creaked up off my knees, I crawled into bed with a heart full of anticipation. So full, I had to get back out of bed and praise Him in advance for whatever He was about to do.

Even though I couldn't see it with my eyes, I knew the enemy had to be stompin' around like— what's that children's book, Rumplestiltskin?— because his evil plan was null and void!

# Chapter 17

Good thing Frank sent me a text Saturday night saying he'd pick me up at nine o'clock, 'cause us going to church on his praising grounds had surely slipped my mind.

I got up extra early so I could get Eunice squared away. She ate a bowl of my healthy cereal while I ran her bath water. While she was taking a bath, I put fresh sheets on her bed, and prepared another dose of Tylenol.

Once she was full, clean, and somewhat drugged, I informed her of the day's agenda. "Today's a big day for us, Eunice."

"I know," she fanned her hand. "I've worn out my stay. The shelter over at the Catholic church is open on Sundays. You can drop me off there."

"Actually, your son is coming to help you today," I spoke in faith.

Her eyebrows momentarily jumped with excitement. Then she sucked in her chin as sadness crept in. "Paul's coming here?"

"Yes, he is. He's gonna help get you situated with this leg problem, and prayerfully everything else," I implied.

"Everything else like what?"

Despite the stirring in my soul, I tried to keep my excitement at a level Eunice could digest. "We'll just take it step by step."

"I don't want to see him. He doesn't want to see me, either," she jabbered. "Won't do any good."

"Can't do no harm, either."

"Oh, yes it can. Sometimes you've got to leave well enough alone," she preached.

"Maybe I *would* leave it alone if you *was* well enough, but you ain't," I returned mildly. "Frank and I should be back from his church around one-thirty. I expect Paul around two-thirty. My son and his family are coming over, so it won't be just me, you, and Paul sitting up looking at each other in the face. You'll have plenty of folk around."

The lines in her forehead smoothed a bit. "Unh."

"I put the roast in the slow cooker at six this morning. You think you can hobble out of bed and turn it on low around noon?"

"I suppose."

"Thank you, sweetie." I patted her arm and rose to leave.

"B," she stopped me.

I pivoted and turned to face her.

"So I can have some idea of what's normal…how often do you talk to your children?"

"Son bugs me about something or another every couple of days. My oldest, Debra Kay, calls me once a week or so. She keeps me in the loop on all the other ones. My second girl, Cassandra—me and her don't talk much. She not much of a talker to nobody, really. She sends cards and pictures of her family. My baby, Otha—me and him used to talk a lot more before Albert died. Him and Son a lot closer now, according to Debra Kay. I know Otha's alive because he forwards email messages like they goin' out of style. Sometimes I send him a reply and we get to talkin' trough the internet. But when he comes over for the holidays, we can't get him to shut up."

Eunice smiled. "It's nice to have a family, huh?"

"Yes, it is."

"That's good, B. You deserve better than me."

"I'm blessed. And so are you. You just don't know it yet," I professed over her life. With a wink, I dismissed myself from her presence.

I rushed to get my own self ready for church. Just before Frank arrived, I called Ophelia and told her I wouldn't be at service today. Didn't want my church family worryin' about me, you know.

"Oh, Ophelia," I remembered, "put on something extra cute today, hear?"

"For what? You bringin' one of Dr. Wilson's colleagues to church or somethin'?" she laughed.

Took everything in me not to give away Pastor's little secret. "Can't you just follow directions sometime, no questions asked?"

"I got to watch you, B. A woman in love is liable to do anything. Never know what to expect."

"Don't worry about what's goin' on in my life. God's got something for you, too." *Lord, help me.* I almost gave it away. "I gotta go. Bye."

No sooner than I rushed off the phone with Ophelia, Son come calling me. "Momma, you cookin' today?"

Look whose child done forgot their manners. "Hello, Son, it's nice to hear your voice, too."

"Oh. Hi. How are you?"

"I'm fine, thank you very much. And yes, I'm cookin'. I made plenty. You all comin' over?"

"Yes. Me and Wanda."

So much for cookin' to last me all week. I certainly wanted to see my son, but there's something about the grands that lifts a grandmother's spirits. "What about Nikki and Cameron?"

"I haven't talked to them in a few days."

"Awww," I sulked, "I wanted to pinch those chubby cheeks. Guess I'll have to settle for yours instead."

"My cheeks are not chubby, Momma."

"Hmph. Looked pretty plump the last time I saw 'em." That was my roundabout way of tellin' him he needed to watch out. With a daddy who had diabetes and circulation problems, you'd think Son would take better care of himself. Then I remembered who *his* Daddy was. Stubborn as any man with an ego—and believe you me, they *all* got one.

My doorbell rang. "I'll see you later."

"What was that? Is somebody there?" Son fussed.

"Yes. It's Frank. I'm going to church with him today."

"Wh...wh...what's the address of the church?" he stammered.

"I don't know and I don't care."

"Momma," he lectured, "you can't go running out with strange men and not telling anybody where you are!"

"Son, you've already met Frank."

"Yeah, he seems alright," he had to agree. "But what if you go missing?"

"I ain't gon' be missin'. Wherever I am, I'll be in God's care. You got to trust me and the God in me. I like Frank. I like him a lot. Matter of fact, I kissed him."

"You what?!"

"Yep. *On the lips*."

Son gasped for air. "Oh my God. That's way too much information."

"And stop usin' the Lord's name in vain."

The doorbell rang again. "See you. Bye."

Tell you one thing, the Father sure knows how to change a person's perspective. I couldn't hardly even look at Frank without wanting to get close enough to smell his aftershave. Even when he wasn't fresh from the morning, there's something about a man's presence that can't nobody duplicate. In the eight years since Albert died, I'd forgotten how a real man changes the atmosphere.

"Shall we?" Frank held out his hand as we walked toward the front entrance of his church.

Without a word, I allowed him to hold mine the rest of the way.

The building had traditional red brick with stained glass windows and a white steeple. But from the looks of the people filing into the sanctuary, I could tell this wasn't no traditional church. Frank went to one of them 500-member come-as-you-are churches, where folk wear whatever they want. Women in pants, men in jeans, kids might as well be in their play clothes. I should have known Frank would be a member of such a church.

*Lord, keep me from lookin' at what folks got on.*

Everybody at New Direction called Frank "Doc" and they all seemed to be messin' with him the same way my church members did me. They gave him private smiles, happy to see him with somebody, I guessed. Most of them seemed pleasantly surprised to see him with me, but it seemed a few of them had already heard about me. "So good to finally meet you," one of the greeters said as she pointed us closer to the right front section of pews.

*Frank been tellin' people about me?*

The service began with praise and worship. The praise team, dressed in blue and gold robes, sang a bunch of songs I'd never heard of. Thankfully for me, the words popped up on two big screens on either side of the stage. I sure hoped Frank wasn't judging *me* by whether or not I knew them songs because I would have got an F!

The children's dance team performed a routine in the cutest white and hot pink outfits. The littlest one, in the very front, didn't know the moves quite as well as the older ones. Me and Frank elbowed each other as we adored that sweet girl doing her best to praise the Lord in dance. Cute as a bug in a rug!

I stood when the visitors were asked to stand and be recognized. An usher passed me a postcard with information about the church while the announcer gave the usual welcome, followed by a ton of hugs from the church members while the choir sang. If nothing else, Frank's church members were sure friendly.

After another number from the choir and the offering, Frank's pastor took the podium, adjusting the microphone to accommodate his short stature. "Good morning, saints of The Most High. Turn with me to Colossians chapter three."

All over the building, folks started taking out their Bibles. Frank pulled out a two-ton Bible from his Bible bag. Now, of course, his Bible case was big, but I figured he had a pad of paper, some pens, and maybe a few church programs in the brown leather carrier.

*Lord Jesus, is he part-blind?*

Frank set it on his right knee, which was right next to my left. Then he opened it, letting one side rest on me. As he flipped through, I noticed he done been writing a book in The Book—notes, dates, names. So much highlighting, his Bible could have been mistaken for a coloring book. He got all kind of tape throughout, too, holding it together. Made my Bible look like I just got saved last week!

Now, I know better than to judge somebody by their Bible. Ophelia don't believe in writing in hers. She write all her notes on separate paper. But I know good and well your Bible don't get *that* to' up and worn out without some of the Word getting into you.

I suddenly wished Frank would give me his Bible so I could go through and read all his notes, but I guess that might be like asking somebody to read their diary.

Already, I started envisioning me and Frank sitting up to the wee hours of the night talking, pouring over the word. Praying. Sharing. Maybe even passionate debating. I could spend hour upon hour in the word.

Now, I don't want y'all to think I'm being nasty. I'm gon' lay it out like this for you, though: Can't nothin' light my fire like a man who loves the word of the Lord.

Frank's pastor preached on what it means to be dead to the flesh and alive in Christ. He refreshed my soul with his thoughts about life in the Spirit. "Your walk with God shouldn't be a burden. If it is, you need to lay yourself at Christ's feet. Exchange your cross for His. He said in Matthew eleven and thirty that His yoke is easy. His burden is light."

Frank leaned toward me and whispered in my ear, "Wish somebody had told me this forty years ago."

"Me, too." Being raised partly in the holiness church, I thought my salvation was all up to me. I didn't know the Lord was such a good keeper until I came to the end of myself. That's a whole nother story. Suffice it to say, sinking into your holiness is a whole lot easier than fighting the flesh every moment.

Frank's pastor left us with some questions and verses to look up throughout the week as we continued in our personal Bible study. I liked that. Seem like he was going to leave the rest of the teaching up to the Holy Spirit. He the best teacher we got, anyhow.

I asked Frank to take me to the store so I could get some soda pop to go with dinner. With Son coming over, we'd need more than tea.

Frank waited for me to whip in and out, then we were on our way back to my house. "You eatin' with us, right?"

He angled his head away from me and winced. "I...I don't think so."

"Why not?"

He shook his head, his cheeks pinched. "It's Eunice. I'm...uncomfortable around her because—"

"I know, Frank," I rescued him from the saddle of speaking ill of Eunice. "I heard what she said to you the other night. She's got a bad habit of sabotagin' relationships with people. I done decided to forgive her and treat her right, regardless."

Frank's features returned to normal. "Okay. As long as we *both* know what's going on, I'm fine."

*Lord, thank You for solving that awkward moment. We need your help with all the other ones on the way today.*

# Chapter 18

"Eunice, we're home!"

Frank detoured to the kitchen to put the sodas in the icebox. I called again, "Eunice!"

No answer. I rapped on the door. "Eunice?"

Still no answer. Slowly, I turned the knob and found the bed empty. Made, but empty. *Good Lord! She done run off again!*

I dashed back to the kitchen. "Frank, she's gone."

"Gone where?"

"I don't know." I checked the dial on the crock pot. It was set to "low," as she'd agreed. I took a fork from the drawer and stuck it in the roast. The meat separated precisely the way it should have after cooling down for a while. "She ain't been gone long."

*Ring!* I rushed to answer my phone. "Hello?"

"B, it's me," Libby's voice came through. "I got a call from Eunice soon as we let out of church. She asked me to pick her up from your house. Said she don't want to see her son."

"Nonsense. I saw the way her eyes lit up when I told her Paul was coming."

"Well, me and Peter went and got her. She demanded we take her to the Catholic shelter, so we dropped her off there. I tried to stall, asked her to eat with us. She wouldn't wait. Said if we didn't take her right then, she'd walk there herself."

"I see. Don't worry. You did the right thing, Libby. We'll get her back."

"Let me know what you need me to do," she offered.

"God's workin' it out. I'll talk to you later."

All Frank could do was watch me work 'cause I didn't have time to explain it to him. Quickly, I opened my call log and dialed Paul. "Paul, this Mrs. Jackson. Just checkin' to make sure you on your way."

"Yes, ma'am. I'll be exiting off the main highway in a few minutes."

Seem like I could breathe again now that I knew he was underway. "Okay. We'll be waiting on you."

If Eunice hadn't acted so you-know-what with Frank, I would have sent him over to the shelter to get her. I couldn't very well go myself, with Son and his family on their way over – not to mention I needed to finish the rolls.

We needed a Plan C. "Frank, when Paul gets here, I'd like for you and him to go over to the Catholic church on Main, get Eunice, and bring her back here."

He crossed his arms and poked out his lips. "We'll do our best."

"Between you, Paul, and the Lord, I'm sure y'all can handle it."

Son and Wanda brought an iced lemon cake. Store-bought, mind you, but it was a nice gesture. "Set it over on the table," I instructed my daughter-in-law after greeting both her and my son with kisses and hugs.

Frank and Son shook hands and took turns sizing each other up with all their manly questions. Asking each other how was business going, what football teams they thought would make it to the Superbowl. Me and Wanda set the table as they carried on with all their stuff.

"He's handsome, Mama B," Wanda complimented me. "And such a gentleman, I can tell."

"Honey, with my Help, I picks 'em good," I bragged in the Lord.

"You raise 'em good, too, Mother."

"Why thank you, sweetheart. Raised 'em to pick good wives, too," I returned the compliment.

I figured Paul would be arriving at any moment, so I called everyone's attention and filled them in on as much of the situation with Eunice and Paul as I felt they needed to know. "Let's pray for God's best between those two."

We heard a car pull into the driveway. Frank and I made our way to the front. Through the sheer curtains, I could see Eunice's son maneuvering things to get out of his van. Lord knows, my driveway wasn't built for nobody with a handicap.

Under my breath, I feared, "Let me go help—"

Frank put a hand on my shoulder. "He's got it, B."

Reminded me of how Albert used to stop me from jumpin' in with our kids all the time. He'd let 'em struggle until they learned how to do things for themselves. Broke my heart to sit there and watch, sometimes, but I believe that's one reason God's plan is for kids to have a Momma and a Daddy if at all possible. Got to balance one another out.

Finally, the doorbell rang. Frank and I answered it together.

I promise on my turkey stew, Eunice couldn't have denied that boy if she wanted to. Same light brown skin, funny little nose, wiry hair. "Hello, Paul! Welcome! Come on in!"

He finagled across the threshold with his steel-lookin' crutches, the kind with a cuff for the arm.

I certainly didn't wish this struggle on him, but I was glad to know he wasn't lying—getting around really wasn't easy for him.

Seemed like he might tilt over any moment to me, so I didn't try to hug on him. "Paul, this is my friend, Frank."

They both nodded at each other and gave simple hello's.

"Come on in. I've got a roast with vegetables and cornbread. We've even got a lemon cake," I did my best to put him in a good mood.

"Smells delicious," he replied as he followed us into the dining area.

"Let me introduce you to my family."

Son and Wanda stood as I called their names. Again, Paul did the best he could to greet them despite his hands being preoccupied. Son offered his seat at the table.

"Oh, no. Actually, it's best if I sit on a couch or someplace soft. I can't sit upright and straight for too long."

We all hopped to his rescue, pointing the way toward the living room. Paul worked his way onto the couch and took a rest, sweat beads forming at his temples. Didn't help that his upper body was carrying so much extra weight. *Lord, bless him.*

"Let me get you some water," Wanda said, turning back toward the kitchen.

"That would be great."

She returned with the water and handed the glass to Paul, who gulped it down quickly. He pushed his glasses back in place. "Thank you."

Now that he'd gotten himself all comfortable, I hated to tell him it was time to get back up. He and Frank had a job to do. "Paul, you and Frank are gonna go get your mother from the Catholic shelter in downtown Peasner."

"I thought she was here," he said with a question mark on his face.

"She was. But she left."

He grumbled. "Doesn't surprise me. I've come all this way for nothing."

Wanda and Son slipped back into the kitchen, leaving me and Frank alone with Paul. Inside, I started praying for the right words to comfort Paul. I done seen so many folk suffer all their lives after the rejection of a mother. I could only imagine what he was goin' through.

"Oh, she's not gone far. You and Frank can get her and bring her back here so she can eat with us," I encouraged him. "Won't take but a minute."

He breathed in like he 'bout tired of foolin' with his Momma. "Might as well get it over with. Let's go."

Paul took hold of his crutches, rocked his behind twice (just like his Momma) and rolled up to a standing position. The whole time, I held my breath because it looked like he might take a tumble at any moment. I could tell this man had been on these crutches for some years, the way he had it down to a science.

Frank led us to the door. "We'll be back in a little while," he told me. And once Paul had made it down the steps, Frank turned back to me and mouthed, "Pray."

He didn't need to ask me again.

# Chapter 19

I asked Son and Wanda to join me as I prayed for the Lord to give Frank the right words to say with Paul, then give Paul and Frank the right words to say with Eunice. Only He knows how to mend a broken heart—two of 'em at once, actually.

After we finished praying, Son said he was starvin' so he made himself a bowl of cereal, to Wanda's dismay. She rolled her eyes at him, then looked at me, and we laughed together at my oldest boy.

They went on into the living room and watched a little TV while we all waited for Frank to get back with our other guests.

I was wiping down the counters when the Spirit thumped my heart again. Seem like my entire body froze. "Speak, Lord. Speak *right now* through Your servant, Frank. I come against confusion from the enemy. In Jesus' name, give him exactly what to say."

\* \* \* \* \*

*"How long have you been in practice?" Paul asked.*

*"A little over thirty years. And you're a judge, right?"*

*"Yes. Second year. Practiced law privately for three years. Before that, worked for the state."*

*"Quite impressive, especially at your age. B says your mother is very proud of you," Frank ventured carefully.*

*"I don't see how she can be proud, she had nothing to do with my achievements," he smoldered.*

*"Were you born after seventy-three?" Frank asked.*

*"Yes."*

*"The way I see it," Frank said, "anybody born after Roe versus Wade ought to be thankful for at least being alive."*

*"I guess. Never thought of it like that," Paul gave up.*

*In his heart, Frank thanked God for a way to relate to Paul through his profession. He knew B must have been praying for him at that moment. He probed further. "Where'd you study?"*

*"Southern Methodist University. How about you?"*

*Frank eased into his history, "I did four years in the military before I went to Southern University, in Louisiana, then—"*

*"What branch of service?" Paul was eager to know.*

*"Navy."*

*"Army," Paul spurted.*

*"Oh," Frank probed further, "Were you injured in combat?"*

*Paul flinched slightly.*

*"Sorry," Frank apologized. "Guess I'm so used to asking people about their medical histories—"*

*"Not a problem, coming from you," Paul gave in to the line of questioning. "I wish I'd been injured in combat. Might be easier to explain. No, my story isn't even close to glamorous or honorable. I'd come home from the military on leave. My mom and my brother, Jared, picked me up from the airport. We had an accident on the way home."*

Frank remembered. "Yeah, B said you'd mentioned an accident. Your brother passed away?"

"Yes." Paul gazed out the passenger's window and Frank turned the corner.

"So sorry to hear that. Drunk driver, I think she said, right?" Frank asked.

Paul quickly swerved his glance toward Frank. "Yes. And apparently she failed to mention that she was the drunk party."

*This news put Frank at a loss for words. How can I respond to Paul's anger? Maybe Eunice deserved to lose her relationship with her son, after all she'd done. Sometimes, it's best to sever the chord and leave people to their own devices.*

*Immediately, Frank recognized those thoughts weren't from the Lord. Any reasoning that leaves somebody alone to wallow in their own guilt went against the gospel of reconciliation.*

Frank decided to cut to the chase with Paul because, being a man of the law, he must have an appreciation for the raw truth. "Look, I haven't walked a day in your shoes, but I know what it's like to lose respect for a parent. My dad's been in prison for most of my life."

"That's where my mom should be," Paul argued. "If I'd been on the bench, I would have locked her up forever. The sentencing judge gave her ten years' probation. Bleeding-heart wuss."

"The judge gave her mercy."

"She didn't deserve to be free again. Serves her right she can hardly find decent housing that'll take her with a criminal record. She shouldn't have gotten mercy…" his voice trailed off.

It was time. "Paul, do you know Christ?"

*Eunice's son cleared his throat. "I'm a member of Calvary Church."*

*Paul had answered the question by not answering it. Suddenly, Frank understood that his most important mission of the day was not to reunite Paul with Eunice. It was to introduce Paul to Christ. As he positioned his car between two yellow lines in the parking lot, Frank thanked God for the privilege of leading another soul home.*

# Chapter 20

I'll probably never know how Paul and Frank managed to talk Eunice into coming back to my house. That's probably none of my business. All I know is, when the three of them came through the door, my heart leapt for joy.

"Welcome back, Miss Houdini," I teased my friend.

She fell into my hug. "You're something else, you know?"

"Come on in."

Wanda and I had moved all the dishes to the living room so we could all sit around Paul and enjoy fellowship with one another while we ate. Even though he and Eunice didn't sit next to one another, they was civil.

We had enough food for everyone to have two servings. That Paul could sure eat! Said he hadn't had home-cooked food like that in a long time. Then Eunice asked him how long it had been since he'd had chicken and dumplings.

Paul closed his eyes like he was trying to remember. "Not since we were at the house."

An awkward silence stood between them.

Everybody in the room held their breath. Not one spoon clanked on a plate.

"I'd be glad to make you some," Eunice offered.

*Move on his heart, Lord.*

Finally, Paul replied real softly, "Okay."

It would probably take some time for them to work through whatever they had goin' on, I could tell.

But I also had a feelin' the Lord had started workin' on both their hearts. Between me prayin' and Frank talkin', He had already done a mighty work.

Son and Wanda said they had to leave, so I packed them plates to take back home.

With the evening coming on soon, Frank said he had to get home and get rest for the week.

"Before you go, can I ask you to kind of give Paul some advice on what we ought to do about Eunice's leg?"

Not quite sure if he'd forgotten or not, but it was still my endeavor to get Eunice moved on to her next habitat. Two grown, strong-minded women wasn't meant to stay in a house together too long, in my book.

"My leg's feeling much better," Eunice chirped.

"Mother, I saw you limping," Paul told the truth. "You're *not* well."

"She needs medical attention. It may be something simple. Or not. Can't tell without a thorough examination," Frank said.

Despite Eunice's protesting, Paul got his mother to agree to see a doctor. Funny how she wouldn't listen to nobody but her own child.

"Thank you, Doctor. For *everything*. I'll make some calls and get someone to look at her as soon as possible. I'll keep in touch." Paul flipped himself up on those crutches again.

"Wait a minute." Eunice helped herself into an upright position. "Paul, I'm leavin' with you if you don't mind dropping me off. There's some really nice people at that shelter, even if they do make you go to church almost every day."

The two of them standin' there was a sight to see. Paul on his crutches, Eunice on her cane. Chile, they both needed each other something awful and didn't even know it yet.

"Eunice, you're welcome to stay here," I said despite my flesh screamin' for me to close my mouth.

"No, B. You've done more than enough. I sure do thank you."

I helped Eunice to my spare bedroom so she could gather her things. Everything she owned fit into four grocery bags and that fanny pack, bless her heart. "You sure about this shelter?"

"I been livin' in and out of different places since my second husband died. Gives me a sense of adventure," she said.

"I ain't tryin' to be all in your business, Eunice, but I believe I know you well enough where I can ask you why you won't just get your own place. You seem to have enough money."

She mumbled, "Mmmmm, yeah. My second husband left me more money than I know what to do with, but I might slow down soon if I find the right place. The money won't last much longer, at the rate I'm going."

"You might want to ask Paul to help you with that," I suggested. "My husband left me in a good place, too. We'er both blessed."

She tied knots in all four of her bags. It pained me to see her leaving my house for the homeless shelter. But I had to settle for the fact that at least Eunice was leaving with a budding relationship with her son. Maybe if she felt like he was worryin' over her the way Son worries over me, she might get settled in order to keep the peace between the two of them. God would have to take it from here.

"You've got a good one in there." She pointed toward the living room.

"So do you," I said. "Paul's real nice. Respectable."

"And Frank's a good man, too." She flopped down on the bed and hung her head. "B, I've got to tell you something."

I had a feeling about what was buggin' her.

"A few nights ago, when you left me and Frank alone, I tried to come on to him. I'm sorry. I don't know why I always have to ruin every good thing that comes to me. I wouldn't blame you if you didn't want to see me again. I just had to say it before you make any kind of commitments to see me or Paul in the future." Her brown eyes looked up at me, filled with tears.

"I knew already, Eunice."

Her mouth gaped open in shock. "Frank told you?"

"No. I heard it for myself," I admitted.

She squinted at me. "You *knew*? And you let me *stay*? Why?"

Finally, the Lord had opened the door for me to witness to Eunice. "Because that's the love of Christ. He loved us when we were His enemies."

A tear rolled down her fattened cheeks. Then she smiled, "They taught me that in church, when I was a little girl. And I really believed Jesus loved me, that he'd died for me."

"No need for you to stop believin' now. He loves you as much now as He did then. He's waiting on you to recognize that He's still right where you left He took up residence—right inside of you."

"You think so?" she asked with a childish wonder.

"He *said* so in His word," I assured her.

She got up quicker than I'd seen her move—well, since the day she whacked Libby with the cane—and held on to me for dear life.

"Thank you, B. Thank you for loving me. I swear, being with you feels like I've been to church."

"The body of Christ *is* the church."

She sniffed, wiped her eyes dry. "Okay. Soon as I get to the church, I'm gonna ask somebody for a Bible and start readin' it again. And I'm gonna look up everything about Jesus and God. And if I have a question, I'll call you, all right? Might even go to church with you. How about for Christmas?"

"Sure thing."

You know, when I think about it, I know it was all God. Folk think every problem between two women got to end up in some kind of screamin', shoutin', scratchin' match. They been watchin' too many reality shows. When the saints let the love of God work it out, love always bring 'em to peace. Always.

And ain't noboby mad about that 'cept the devil.

# Epilogue

*Thanksgiving Day*

You can't imagine what it took to get my children to agree to have Thanksgiving at Frank's house. Debra Kay said she was afraid her grands might break something. Cassandra and Otha didn't want to break tradition. The only one who didn't seem to put up too much fuss was Son, which actually surprised me. But since he the one Frank done seen the most, it made sense.

Anyhow, there wasn't enough room in my house for us all to fellowship comfortably—my kids and Frank's, with his grands, too, so they had to get over it.

Wednesday night, Cassandra's family and Otha and most of the great-grands stayed up all night keeping up all kind of racket. Good racket, though. They hooked up a moving video game on my television—a ree? a wee?—something or another. They even got me on that thing dancing to Michael Jackson while I waited for the cornbread to cook so I could make the dressing.

"Come on, Mama B!" Cameron begged. You know I can't turn him down.

Thursday, we caravanned over to Frank's. His house is halfway between Peasner and Dallas, so it didn't take us too long. His neighborhood is old, with mature trees and large yards. Little over an acre, I'd say.

Plenty room for the kids to run outside and play with his dogs. Plus, he got a fenced in trampoline. He also had a pool, but it was too cool outside for anybody to consider jumping in.

When we pulled through the porte cochere and Cameron got a good look at the back yard, he exclaimed, "Wow! Is Dr. Frank rich?"

"Of course he's rich, Cameron, he's a doctor," Debra Kay's granddaughter, Lexus, answered.

"Man! I'm gonna be a doctor when I grow up," Cameron announced.

We all laughed 'cause everybody knows how sensitive Cameron is to pain. Boy cried like a baby when he stepped on a sticker one time.

Frank greeted us at the front door. He gave me a quick smack on the lips—in front of my people—which sent Cameron and Lexus into a fit of giggles. They so silly.

"Hey, Baby. Happy Thanksgiving," Frank said.

"Same to you," I replied. "Need you to get some more stuff from the car, hon."

The children took off for the back yard, which was fine for a while. Frank and I took a moment to introduce all our kids to one another. Frank's got a son, Frank, Jr. and a daughter. I already knew Eva from back when she used to help at the food pantry.

All the kids seemed scared. Fidgety. Like they was lookin' at a sad movie. I had to remember that they all wished their deceased parent was there instead of me or Frank. We had to give them some time. *Help 'em, Lord.*

All the women—my daughters, Wanda, and Frank's daughter, Eva—got busy preparing things in the kitchen.

Like the rest of Frank's house, the kitchen was spacious enough so plenty of folk had elbow room. I think he said the whole thing was close to thirty-five hundred square feet. Hardwood floors, custom drapes, built-in shelves and cabinets, artwork with little lights shining at the bottom of the frames, all the stuff you'd expect in a doctor's house. But with a woman's eye, I could tell it was a bachelor pad. A little dusty here and there.

Cassandra got close enough to me at the counter to whisper, "He calls you *baby*?"

"Mmm hmm."

"That's pretty sexist, don't you think?" she hissed.

"No. It's fine with me."

She rolled her eyes and left me alone. I left her alone, too. Cassandra always been a sensitive child. I can't tell her to butt out of my business as sharp as I do Son 'cause she would take it to heart.

Took a while, but the uneasiness in the kitchen died down as we finished making preparations. Moving in and out of each other's paths, washing each other's pots, passing spoons, taking tastes of this and adding a pat of that always has been the way women end up bonding. Food bring folk together when nothing else will.

When we finally finished and had the table set with the dishes Frank told us to use, I had to congratulate them. "Ladies, looks like we've done a wonderful job."

They all agreed.

Eva got a little teary-eyed. "We haven't had a big dinner like this here in the house since my mom died. These were her favorite dishes."

Debra Kay put her arm around Eva's shoulder. "I'm so sorry."

"Your mother had lovely taste," I said to Eva.

Eva composed herself. "Yes, she did. Thank you, Mama B, for acknowledging her today."

"Mmm hmmm." I rubbed Eva's arm. I knew what it was to lose a mother, too.

She wiped the last stray tear away. "Should we call in the men and kids?"

"Yes, ma'am," I seconded.

We had a time getting everybody washed up. Cassandra's grandson, Ricky, had done split his britches right up the middle, playing on the trampoline. I had to beg mercy to keep him from gettin' popped. "Cassandra, it ain't his fault he's was growin' like a weed."

Another grandchild spared.

Though we had the kids' tables set up in the kitchen area, everybody gathered around the dining room table for prayer first. There was more food on that table than anybody's eyes could take in, let alone stomachs—turkey, chicken, ham, dressing, macaroni and cheese, sweet potatoes, green beans. You name it, we just about had it.

Me and Frank stood at the head, with all our family gathered around, holding hands. Once we were all in place, I bowed my head, waiting for Frank to bless the food.

"Wait a second," Frank brought things to a halt. "Before we say the prayer, there's something I'd like to say."

I opened my eyes and looked up at him. The room fell silent.

"Actually, it's more something I'd like to *ask*." Next thing I knew, Frank was gliding down to one knee.

All the women in the room whooped and hollered. The kids whispering, "What's happening? What is he doing?"

Matter of fact, my first thought was, "Did his knee give out on him?"

That was, until he flipped open a red box and presented me with a ring. Three round-cut diamonds and smaller ones on the shank. Shining like he spent a pretty penny, but dainty enough to fit my style. Chile, this man had been studyin' me.

"Beatrice, will you marry me?"

My eyes blurred up with tears that fell onto his hands. "Yes, Frank. I'll marry you."

He grabbed the handle on a chair and pushed himself back into a standing position, both knees popping.

"Be careful, honey," I cautioned.

He was slow gettin' back up, but once he did, we hugged, rocking back and forth while all grands and great-grands got to hoppin' and hollerin' and the adults clapped.

"I love you, B."

"I love you, too, Frank."


The dinner was lovely. Everybody ate 'til they couldn't eat no more, and then took some home. The menfolk surprised us by cleaning up after everybody. Now *that's* a new tradition I could sure get behind.

My kids headed back to my house. Me and Frank decided we wanted to get out together for a spell and see some of our friends. Plus, we needed a moment to ourselves.

I said my good-bye's to Eva, Frank, Jr., and the rest of my future in-laws.

We were still stuffed when we rolled into his car and took the highway back to Peasner. Ophelia had already invited us to drop by since they were eating late. And by "they", I mean her family, Henrietta's small family, and Pastor.

On the way to Ophelia's, I quizzed Frank about how long he had been planning this, how he knew my ring size, everything a woman wants to know when she gets engaged.

Turns out, a lot of them knew of Frank's intentions already, and that was only right, seeing as he was gonna ask me to marry him in the house their mother picked out and decorated.

He'd gotten Son's blessing ahead of time, too. Not that he needed Son's approval, but that's one thing about Frank: He do things real respectful-like. He honors people, and that makes people honor him in return.

I'm just surprised the secret didn't make it back to me beforehand.

"I had help," he admitted. "Debra Kay is all in your business, you know?"

"She sure is," I had to agree.

The trees lining the highway displayed the most magnificent fall colors; hues only God Himself could have arranged for our eyes to see. "Look at those trees. God is amazing," I gawked.

"Wonderful," Frank added, "awesome." His hand slipped across the console, pulling mine into a comfortable clasp.

I used my free hand to check out the notification from my phone. It was a text from Paul. I opened it to find a picture of him and Eunice sitting at a table. "Me and my mom," was the caption. Brought tears to my eyes yet again as I shared it with Frank.

He stole a quick glance at my phone's screen. "Wow. That's wonderful."

"Mmm hmm. We make a pretty good team in the Lord if I do say so myself."

He squeezed my hand in agreement.

Unfortunately, the closer we got to Ophelia's the more I felt an attitude licking up my spine. Henrietta. I knew she was gon' have somethin' negative to say about the engagement.

"Let me go on and apologize ahead of time for whatever Henrietta might say," I said as we walked toward Ophelia's porch. "I don't know why she's made it her life's goal to make me miserable."

"I've seen it a thousand times, B. When someone is sick or hurting or not completely in their right mind, they take out all their anger and frustration on the person they know loves them and won't reject them. It's human nature," he explained. "Take it as a compliment."

On Frank's advice, I ignored Henrietta's snide remarks as best as I could. We didn't really sit down and give her a chance to go all in, just stood up in the living room where they was all seated and announced the engagement.

After all the huggin', you know Ophelia's question. "When y'all gon' tie the knot?"

"We ain't got that far yet," I covered.

But Frank voiced, "The sooner the better."

"Fast as hotcakes," Henrietta gibbered.

I took a deep breath, walked over to Henrietta and threw the biggest bear hug she ever did get. "I love you and there ain't nothin' you can do about it, you hear?"

Her eyes got all bugged out. That caught her off guard. She didn't have nothin' else smart to say. Ha!

We didn't stay long because it was getting dark already. The drive back to my house was short, but long enough for me to take a long, hard stare at the man sitting across from me and think about the future we would have together. We had a lot to work through, I knew. Like whose house was we gon' live in, whose church we gon' go to, how to change up the wills and so forth. Gettin' married at our age ain't as easy as folk think it is if you got two pennies to rub together.

But I wasn't worried. Just like Frank always said, God works everything out for those who love Him. And we *both* certainly did.

### THE END

***Were you blessed by this book?***
*Please take a few seconds to share your thoughts on any of the Mama B books by leaving reviews online.*
*Thank you sooooo much!*
*-Michelle Stimpson*

# A Note from the Author

*This Mama B series has sparked a new desire to fellowship with believers and share the gospel in the same ways Mama B does—not by preaching at people but by letting Christ be known in the way I treat others. I pray that her example of a godly woman will encourage you to think about how you want to be after walking with the Lord for 40+ years.*

*If you have yet to start your journey in Christ, let me encourage you to seek Him. Seek Him in all of his glory, all of His love, and His wisdom. If you feel the tug in your heart, Thank Him for His goodness, ask Him for forgiveness, and invite Him to live in you. He stands knocking on the door of your heart and is more than pleased to come in and be your Lord (Rev. 3:20). And as both Mama B and I can testify to, He is a good Lord indeed!*

*God bless you!*
*-Michelle Stimpson*

Did You Read Mama B Books 1 & 2?
If not, DON'T WORRY! You can still enjoy Mama B
dealing with her friends, family, and church members
without ruining any surprises.

**Mama B - A Time to Speak (#1)**

The good folks at Mt. Zion Baptist are doing their
best to keep the church flowing smoothly while
Pastor Phillips takes time off to be with his wife in
her final days. Beatrice "Mama B" Jackson even
opens her home so that the women's groups can
continue to meet faithfully after some "rascal" stole
the copper from the church's air conditioning unit.
With her semi-estranged granddaughter and great-
grandson staying in the guest room, Mama B soon has
a full house.

When the interim preacher and his wife start touting
messages that don't line up with the Bible, Mama B
can only take so much of this foolishness. Soon
enough, she realize that there is much more at stake
than she or anyone else at Mt. Zion ever imagined.
It's time to speak.

## Mama B – A Time to Dance (#2)

Mama B thought her life would return to normal, but when her nephew, Derrick, comes knocking on her door, she has to reconsider. Though she's not known for housing marital fugitives, she realizes Derrick is looking for more than a place to stay; he needs help finding his way back to God.

Of course, help is almost Mama B's middle name until Henrietta crosses the line with her accusations about Mama B's intentions with the recently widowed pastor. Mama B isn't looking for romance with either the pastor or her suitor, Dr. Wilson—but will love come looking for her?

**Order Online Now!**

## About the Author

In addition to her work in the field of education, Michelle ministers through writing and public speaking. Her works include the highly acclaimed *Boaz Brown, Divas of Damascus Road* (National Bestseller), and *Falling Into Grace,* which has been optioned for a movie of the week. She has published several short stories for high school students through her educational publishing company.

Michelle serves in women's ministry at her home church, Oak Cliff Bible Fellowship. She also ministers to women and writers through her blog. She regularly speaks at special events and writing workshops sponsored churches, schools, book clubs, and educational organizations.

The Stimpsons are proud parents of two young adults and one crazy dog.

## Other Books by Michelle Stimpson

**Fiction**
Boaz Brown
Divas of Damascus Road
Falling into Grace
I Met Him in the Ladies' Room (Novella)
Last Temptation (Starring "Peaches" from *Boaz Brown*)
Mama B: A Time to Speak (Novella)
Mama B: A Time to Dance (Novella)
Someone to Watch Over Me
The Good Stuff
Trouble In My Way (Young Adult)

**Non-Fiction**
Did I Marry the Wrong Guy? And other silent ponderings of a fairly normal Christian wife

Uncommon Sense: 30 Truths to Radically Renew Your Mind in Christ

Visit Michelle online:
www.MichelleStimpson.com
www.Facebook.com/michelle.stimpson2
http://www.TheWifeAcademy.com

Made in the USA
Lexington, KY
18 August 2016